THE GREAT WIDE SEA

M. H. HERLONG

SCHO

New York Toronto

Mexico City New De

ISBN-13: 978-0-545-20322-7
ISBN-10: 0-545-20322-8

12 11 10 9 8 7 6 5 4 3 2 1   9 10 11 12 13 14/0

Printed in the U.S.A   40

First Scholastic printing, October 2009

Set in Goudy
Book design by Jim Hoover

In memory of
Stephen Marlowe,
my teacher

GERRY SAYS HE remembers the sun and the fish. All the fish. The silver ones swimming around the rudder at anchor. The brilliant blue ones flashing across the fiery red coral. The big black ones curving like shadows at our bow as we sailed with the Gulf Stream.

But the one he remembers best, he says, is the first one he stabbed with his spear. He tells how he shoved the spear down right into the flounder's head, how he pulled the still-struggling fish from the water, and how he laughed—because he was six years old and could kill a fish.

He remembers all that, he says, but nothing more. He says he was too little when it happened. He says I have to tell him stories.

So I do.

Once upon a time there was family. Then a boat. And then islands.

Once upon a time three boys were lost at sea. One almost drowned. One almost went crazy. One fell off a cliff.

Gerry says I'm making it up, but I'm not. Everything I tell him is the truth. I just don't tell him everything.

I don't tell about the morning we woke up and Dad was gone. I don't talk about the storm. Or when we wrecked on the coral reef. I don't talk about—I never will talk about—when I left Gerry alone, standing there on the empty beach of that desert island with Dylan dying at his feet.

I don't tell stories about those things and I don't need to. Because Gerry is lying. He remembers it all. Sometimes when we go sailing now we watch the shore slip by and we remember together. Not with words or even looks but with blood rhythm—with the rush of electricity from one body to another. I pull in the mainsheet. I lean on the tiller. I tighten the jib. The boat flies.

And I don't need to tell stories. I sit close to my brothers on the rail and I get dizzy. Like when you stump your toe and it hurts so bad you think you'll faint. The world spins backwards. I lose my place in my life. I'm running and I don't know if I'll make it in time. Then it's all starting over again. And it's not a story at all. It's real and I am fifteen.

THE BOAT

CHAPTER ONE

WE DROVE ALL night to get to the boat. I kept asking Dad to stop and let us sleep, but he always said, "No, I want to get a little farther," until Gerry fell asleep leaning against the door, his mouth open and drooling, and Dylan tilted over sideways on the backseat. Somewhere south of Miami, we pulled over at an all-night gas station.

"Dad, please," I said when we got back in the car.

"It's too late," he said, and drove us back onto the dark highway.

So I just sat there for hours, watching us rush into the hot, muggy June night and thinking about the spiky palm trees and mosquitoes and strange, quick lizards scuttling off into the crumbling asphalt along the edge of the road. When we finally made the Keys, my head was aching and the sun was just rising behind us.

"Look." It was Dylan's voice. "The morning star."

I looked. Dylan was barely eleven, but he knew about stars. One star hung there in the sky, still bright enough to be seen in the first light of morning.

"It's Venus," Dylan said.

I closed my eyes, waiting for Dad to start some story or recite some poem, but he didn't. He didn't say anything. Even the way he looked had completely changed. He had wrinkles around his eyes. The gray in his hair shone in the dim morning light.

I shifted in my seat to see Dylan. "It's not a star," I said. "It's a planet."

Gerry stirred in the backseat. "It *is* a star," he said, wiping his face with Blankie.

"You're only five," I said, turning back around in my seat. "What do you know?"

"Dylan says it's a star," Gerry said firmly. "And Dylan knows better than you."

"Be quiet," Dad said. "All of you."

I pressed my forehead against the cool glass of the car window and stared out at the gray ocean. I still couldn't believe it. One day he had just announced we were going sailing for a year. A whole year. "Like on the lake, Ben," he had said. "You'll love it."

"I won't love it."

"But you love sailing."

"I want a car. Mom said I could get a car when I turned sixteen. Five months and I'm supposed to get a car."

"That's not important anymore."

"It *is* important. She said—"

"Enough," he'd said. "Just stop."

I had stopped. What difference did it make what I said? He had already decided.

In Key West, Dad found us a room in a motel near the marina where the boat was docked. Gerry curled up on one bed, holding Blankie bunched in front of his face. I stretched out next to him. Dylan made a pallet on the floor. Dad had the second bed all to himself. I lay watching his still profile backlit through the curtains. Suddenly he sat up trembling and covered his eyes. Then he stood, wiped his face with his shirt-tail, and picked his way through the litter on the floor to step outside and close the door quietly behind him.

I eased out of bed and opened the curtain a tiny bit to look out. Our window faced the parking lot, but I could see a scrap of the marina if I pressed my cheek against the glass. Dad was right. I did love to sail. He and I had explored the lake together for hours, just the two of us. By the time I was twelve, he had let me go out alone on the twenty-two-footer we kept on the lake. For the last year, I didn't even have to ask. I knew all the coves in the lake. I knew the shallows and the deep trench running through the middle. I loved to sail. But I also loved to come home, and this time we weren't coming home.

I climbed back into the bed, but I couldn't sleep. Maybe it was the way Dylan slept so soundly, not moving at all. Or maybe it was the little sniffing, crying noises Gerry was making. He had dropped Blankie on the floor, and his thin, careful fingers were searching for it in his sleep. As I reached to pick it up, he suddenly rose up on his knees, his hair sweaty, his eyes wide open.

"Mom?" he called. *"Mom?"*

I sat up in front of him, but he looked through me.

"Mom!" His voice went shrill. "Mom!"

I touched Blankie lightly to his face. "Gerry," I said, "wake up."

He turned slightly and saw me. His face crumpled. He took Blankie.

"Ben," he whispered. Then he flopped over and curled into a ball facing the wall.

"Are you okay?" I asked.

He jerked his head in a quick nod and covered his face with Blankie.

I looked up and there was Dad, standing halfway in the door.

"He was crying again?" Dad asked.

I didn't say anything. I just lay down beside Gerry and shut my eyes. After a minute or two, Dad left. I wished I could shut my ears too. Why did I have to hear every sound? The maid's cart scraping from room to room. Cartoons on the TV next door. Gerry still whimpering a little. And Dylan so utterly quiet.

I felt as if I hadn't slept in months, as if I had lain in my bed every night, my mind filling up with things while I stared at the stars Dylan and Mom had stuck on the ceiling of our room two summers ago. If I was lucky, my mind would eventually start playing the tapes of a story I liked to tell myself, like the one about the car I was going to get. If I was not lucky, my mind would start playing the other tapes.

In that motel room, my mind started playing the other tapes—over and over. And the first scene was always the same. My mind saw the phone just before it was going to ring. It was lying beside Dad on the sofa, white against the dark blue. I knew it was going to ring, and I couldn't stop it.

It was April, early afternoon, and Dad and I were watching the ball game together on TV. Our team was ahead, but the game was slow and I felt sleepy. Gerry had already fallen asleep on the sofa, his hair still damp from his swimming lesson. Dylan was upstairs. His birthday was next month and he was studying telescope catalogs. At least that's what he told me later.

Mom had left in the car about twenty minutes before to get ice cream.

Then the phone rang.

Sometimes when you read a book or watch a TV show, you see the people and you think, *Don't do that. Don't open that door. Don't answer that phone.* You know everything is about to change. "Stop!" you want to say. "Rewrite the story. Rewind the tape. Don't let it happen that way." But you can't. The people always open the door or answer the phone. The bad thing always happens, and there is nothing you can do about it.

So Dad answered the phone.

"Yes?" he said. Then, "Yes," again. "Oh, my God." A longer pause. "Of course. Right away."

He put the phone down.

Everything had changed and there was nothing we could do about it.

Two blocks away, a guy had run a red light. He had killed Mom. Her clothes were still in her closet. Her lotions were still in the bathroom. You could still smell her little sachet things when you walked into the bedroom.

But Mom was gone.

I felt like slamming my fist through the motel ceiling above me. I felt like I had bad breath. I felt like I stank. I felt if I didn't sleep soon, I'd explode like a white-hot star, and everything would disappear—Florida, the boat, my brothers, and Dad, everything—sucked into the deep, black hole that was me.

CHAPTER TWO

MY MOM'S NAME was Christine Emily Byron and this is what I can tell you about her. The last time I hugged her, I was exactly as tall as she was. Your own mom always seems so big, and then one day you have this shock of realizing you are as tall as she is. Then you see that after all she is small.

Mom had dark hair that she always kept in a ponytail. She wore jeans, never skirts. She took care of the house and she worked in the garden and she teased Dad, especially when he quoted poetry at us. Like, maybe we'd be taking a walk in the woods by the lake in the fall and Dad would stop and sweep his arms toward the trees and say, "'Margaret, are you grieving over Goldengrove unleaving?'" And Mom would say, "Jim, how many times do I have to tell you—my name is Christine."

When Mom died, everyone wanted to help. Dad's sister flew down. The other professors at the university took over Dad's classes. My friend Andrew even wanted to take me to a game, but I didn't go. I stayed at home with my brothers while Dad sat in the dark and read poems. He'd be quiet for a while and then read us a line. "Listen to this, boys," he would say. "'Do not go gentle into that good night. Rage, rage against the dying of the light.'" Then he would cover his face with his hands. After a while he would say, "Isn't it time for you guys to be in bed?" So we went to bed and we didn't come back downstairs. We didn't want to surprise him. It was too easy to catch him crying.

When it was time to dress for the funeral, he went into his room and shut the door. Usually he helped with our ties, but this time I had to do it for everyone. When we were walking to the car, he stopped and looked at us.

"Did you tie your own ties?" he asked.

"Ben did it," Gerry said.

"He did a good job," Dad said, then rubbed Gerry's head.

"You messed up his hair," I said.

"He didn't," Gerry said.

"Not much," Dylan said quietly.

"I like it this way." Gerry held his hands over his head.

"Be quiet," Dad said. "All of you. Get in the car."

We got in the car, and I sat in the front seat. *Mom's seat,* I thought, and closed my eyes. When we got home, I was so tired I wanted to go straight to bed, but all these people were at our house, standing around talking in low voices and eating sandwiches. I went to the kitchen, and there was Aunt Sue, loading another platter.

"Where's Dad?" I asked her.

"He's upstairs."

"He belongs down here."

"He'll be down soon," she said, and put her arm around my shoulders. She squeezed me a little, then stepped away. "Give him time, Ben. He'll be all right."

I picked up one of the sandwiches. "It's not fair," I said, and squashed the sandwich in my hand.

"Ben! Don't do that." She unrolled my fingers, took out the sandwich, and dropped it in the trash. She handed me a cloth to clean my hand, then picked up the platter of sandwiches and left.

I wiped my hand and turned to lean my forehead against the refrigerator. It was cool and vibrated slightly. It would have been good, I thought, to disappear right then. To disintegrate. Then the refrigerator cycled off. I stood up straight and turned around. Gerry was standing in the kitchen looking at me. He held Blankie bunched up against his mouth. He lowered it a little. "Are you okay, Ben?"

I nodded.

"I'm okay, too," he said.

I sat in a chair and pulled him into my lap. He leaned his head against my shoulder. That close up, I could smell Blankie. It smelled like sleeping and yesterday and all our lives before today.

I picked up a corner and pressed it to my nose.

"It smells good, doesn't it," Gerry said, and I nodded.

CHAPTER THREE

THAT FIRST MORNING in Key West I woke up with Blankie half under my head and Gerry breathing in my face. Dylan was looking out the window. When I sat up, he turned toward me.

"Dad's gone to see the boat and do some shopping at the marina store," he said.

"Great," I said. "What time is it?"

"Lunchtime," he answered.

We called for pizza. When I ate the last piece, I balled up my napkin and tossed it in a perfect arc into the trash can. "Three points," I said. Dylan smoothed his napkin on his thigh. I grabbed it and tossed it in too. "Three points again. The champ rules!"

Nobody said anything.

"What is the name of this boat again?" I asked.

"*Chrysalis*," Dylan said.

"Does it mean anything?" Gerry asked. He threw his napkin. It fell on the floor.

"It's a scientific term," Dylan said. "It's the cocoon stage of a butterfly or moth."

Gerry picked up his napkin, sat down, and threw again. He missed again.

"Then why don't they just say 'cocoon'?" Gerry asked, and tried his napkin again. Missed. It fell on the bed.

"Sounds like a girl's name," I said. "Should be a perfume or something like that."

Gerry picked up his napkin, threw it again, and missed. "Sounds like Mom's name to me," he said.

"For Pete's sake!" I snatched up the napkin and threw it toward the trash can. "Make the shot, will you!" But I threw too hard. The napkin sailed right over the trash can and fell on the floor.

"Missed," Gerry said.

"Shut up." I lay back on the bed. I closed my eyes.

Wind Racer, I thought. Now that was a good name. Or *Sea Hawk. Wave Dancer* or *Free Time* or *Summer Dream.* All of them were good names. All of them were much better than *Chrysalis.* Even no name at all would be better than that.

The boat we had sailed on the lake at home didn't have a name. We just called it "the boat," and we sailed it every chance we got. Dad even talked about sailing it around the world. When I was little, I believed him. He made up stories about sailing through tsunamis and living off the land in Tahiti. We read *Kon-Tiki* and *Dove* and *Alone Around the World*. Then after Mom was pregnant the last time, he didn't talk about it anymore. I decided he had never really meant it, and I was glad, because I wanted to play baseball and go to summer camp and get a car.

But he had meant it, and he did not forget.

About two months after Mom died, we got home from school one afternoon to see a FOR SALE sign in the yard. "Don't worry," I told Dylan and Gerry. "This house will never sell. Mom always said it was too small."

That night I called for Chinese again and the guy brought all the wrong stuff. I was just starting to make Gerry a peanut butter sandwich when Dad came home.

"I guess you guys saw I listed the house for sale," he said. "I was going to tell you first. I didn't know the sign would go up so fast."

"Why would you want to sell the house?" I asked.

"It's a surprise," he said. "I'll explain over dinner. Sit down."

"I'm making Gerry a sandwich."

"Gerry has to learn to eat what's on the table," Dad said. "When we're on the boat, our diet will be very limited."

We all looked at Dad, but he just kept on serving himself.

"Boat?" I finally asked.

"That's the surprise," he said. "But first, presents." He

pulled three books out of his briefcase, set them beside his plate, and then handed me the one on top. *Boat Engine Basics,* it read, *With an Emphasis on the Most Common Diesel Models in Use Today.*

"Ben," he said. "You like cars. Your job is to learn about engines, particularly diesel engines.

"Dylan," Dad continued, "you like the stars. You can learn navigation." He gave Dylan the next book. *Navigation* was all the title said. Dylan took the book and smoothed the top with the palm of his hand.

"Gerry," Dad said. "Every boat needs crew. You can be crew." The last book was a kid's picture book: *Sailing for Children.* Gerry's chin started to quiver.

"It's okay, Gerry," Dad said. "I'll tell you a story. Once upon a time there was a man named Jim and his three sons. They loved to sail."

"I don't like to sail," Gerry whispered.

"That's because you don't know how," Dad said. "You will when you learn." He went on with his story. "One day, they all went to live on a sailboat."

"Dad," I interrupted, "this is a stupid story."

"Okay, Ben." He breathed deeply. "It's not a story. It's the truth. I'm going to buy a sailboat. I'll be captain, you'll be crew, and we'll all go sailing. For a whole year."

"Dad," I said. "We can't afford that."

"That's what I've been getting to," he said. "We can if we sell the house."

I stared down into my empty plate. I saw I had the flowered plate that had been Mom's favorite. "But what about your job?" I asked. "You can't take a year off."

"Yes, I can," Dad said. "My department head thinks it's a great idea. 'Go,' he said. 'Relax. See some of the world.' And you guys get to miss a whole year of regular classes. I'll be your teacher. No schedules. No deadlines. For twelve whole months."

"But what about the boat on the lake?" I asked.

"Oh, we'll sell that too. It has to be cared for. And besides, we'll have the good ship *Chrysalis*."

"The good ship *Chrysalis*?" Dylan asked.

"*Chrysalis*," Dad repeated. "She's docked in Florida and she's going to be ours. It's like Christmas in June, boys—a big, beautiful sailboat and a year to cruise the Bahamas." He paused and took a long breath. "Everybody I've talked to thinks it's a great idea."

"But you haven't talked to everybody," I said.

"Who else?" Dad asked.

"Us," I said. "You haven't talked to us."

CHAPTER FOUR

WHEN DAD GOT back from the marina store, he couldn't stop talking. He had seen *Chrysalis*. "Get up," he said. "Get moving. We're going sailing right now." The owner was already waiting for us when we got to the boat. Dad hopped right on board and shook his hand, but Dylan, Gerry, and I just stood on the dock and stared.

Dad was wrong. *Chrysalis* was not big or beautiful. She was only a few feet over thirty. Her white hull was scratched and dull, with a long red streak running almost the whole length of the port side. Sun and salt had bleached and roughened the teak. The joints were caked with black gunk. And there on the stern was her name, *Chrysalis*, in fancy, looping letters. It was awful.

Dylan and I finally climbed on board, but Gerry wouldn't

move. "Come on," I said, but he just stood there holding Blankie until I lifted him over the lifelines onto the deck. Down below, Dad and the owner hunched over the radio. "Open the hatches," Dad said without looking around. Dylan and I went to work while Gerry planted himself on the starboard settee, his legs drawn up under him and Blankie bunched over his mouth.

I opened the hatch in the head, but it was too small to air out the tiny, damp closet that doubled as a toilet and shower. Then I helped Dylan, who was struggling with the corroded latch on the large, overhead hatch above the forward V-berth. Several big orange sail bags lay piled on the berth mattress. The biggest sail, the number one genoa, was hanging half out of its bag. The smallest, the working jib, wasn't in a bag at all, and the spinnaker bag had rolled onto the floor. I picked it up and threw it on the pile.

Back in the main cabin, the owner knelt on the floor to lift up the hatch in the cabin sole and show Dad the bilge pump. Dad sat at the navigation table, handling a set of parallel rules, a compass, and several pencils. "Check the quarter berths," he told us.

The quarter berths were two long, narrow sleeping tunnels lying aft of the cabin and tucked in on either side of the center engine compartment. You got in by crawling—headfirst or feetfirst, depending on how you wanted to stay, because once you were in, you couldn't turn around very easily. I crawled headfirst into the starboard quarter berth, opened the single hatch, then lay still on the damp mattress and looked out at the little square of marina I could see through the opening. Dad and the owner were talking sailboats. Waterline and draft. Rigging and sails. Engine and stowage. I tried not to listen, but then Dad started calling for me.

"I'm here." I inched slowly out of the stuffy berth.

The cabin was empty except for Dad. He stood with one foot on the companionway ladder. "It's time to take her out," he said.

"Wait, Dad," I said. He turned to me. "This boat is old," I said, "and dirty."

"We can clean it."

"The engine—"

"You can tune it."

"The sails."

"We'll replace some. Come on. Let's go."

Then he turned and was up the ladder and I was alone in the cabin. When the engine rumbled, I finally followed him topsides. We took *Chrysalis* through every point of sail. We even raised the spinnaker, swinging the huge blue-and-pink sail out on its own pole and rocking along behind it, like the basket dangling underneath a hot-air balloon. After several hours, we dropped the sails, turned on the engine, and motored back. When I killed the engine, I turned to Dad again.

"Dad," I said. "This is crazy. Take us home."

But he didn't hear. He was already following the owner to the dock. They stood talking and gesturing, pointing up at the mast and bending down to check the waterline.

Dylan went back down below and sat at the navigation table, feeling around under the hinged lid, as if he might find something important. Gerry and I sat in the cockpit in the glaring afternoon sun and dripped sweat. Finally, I lay down and closed my eyes. The sun burned red against my eyelids. Diesel fumes filled the air. Engines snarled.

Gerry started swinging his feet, thumping them rhythmically against his seat. "I'm hot," he whined.

"Fan yourself," I said.

"Mosquitoes are biting me."

"Swat them."

"You're being mean," he said, and turned away. He drew his knees up under his chin and hugged his legs. "You're mean and I don't like you anymore."

"So hate me," I said. "I don't care."

I opened my eyes again and looked up. Dad was standing on the dock holding a set of keys in his hand. The owner was walking away.

"I hate you and I hate this boat and I want to go home," Gerry said.

"You're there, Gerry," I said. "This is home now."

CHAPTER FIVE

I HAD TOLD DAD over and over I didn't want to leave home. I wanted to spend the summer alone. I didn't want to talk to anybody. I just wanted to sleep, ride my bike to the lake, and sail away. I wanted to stay gone all day and then come home late, take a long shower, and go back to bed. But Dad wasn't listening. About a month after the sign went up in the yard, he brought home four big duffel bags.

"For our gear," he said.

"Dad," I said. "You can't get a year's worth of gear in one duffel bag!"

"We'll manage with what we can fit," he said, "and it would be best to do it today."

"Today!" I said.

Then he handed Gerry a little-kid CD player and five little-kid CDs. "These will be fun," he said to Gerry.

"When are we leaving?" Dylan asked.

"Not until the day after tomorrow. But the movers are coming tomorrow, and it will be too confusing to try to pack while they're here."

"Movers?" I asked. "What movers?"

"The people who pack up our stuff," Dad said. "The new family won't move in for another month, but I want to be here while our stuff is packed."

"The house sold?" I asked.

"And the boat too," Dad said. "They wanted both."

Dylan stood in the door. Gerry held the new CDs glistening in their cellophane packages.

"You really did it," I said. "You sold the boat and Mom's house too."

"I'm going to pack now," Dad said, and carried a bag to his room.

The next morning, the movers came early and started hauling out the furniture and packing everything else into boxes. Dad kept walking around saying, "We don't need that. Throw it away. Give it to charity." He tossed out all his sailing magazines and about ten years' worth of poetry journals. He put all the baby gear from the attic in a pile for the Salvation Army. He added the tricycles from the garage and a baby swing from the shed. Then I saw him rolling Mom's bike to the giveaway pile.

"Hey, Dad," I said, "that's Mom's."

"I know," he said, and kept walking. He propped it up

against all the old baby gear, squeezed the back tire, jiggled the baby seat on the back, and left it there.

The sun caught the chrome on the handlebars. I closed my eyes against the flash and saw Mom holding up the bike while Gerry sat in the baby seat. She was leaning down to kick up the kickstand, and we were all waiting for her to come. I was thinking about the lake and how cool it was under the trees and how Mom always took so long to get ready to go anywhere. Then she looked up and smiled and said, "Ready." I opened my eyes. The sun had moved. The chrome wasn't shining anymore. I went inside.

The movers were emptying the family room bookshelves into boxes marked FAM RM. Gerry's drawing of our boat on the lake. My cheetah sculpture from kindergarten. Dylan's fourth-grade honor-roll certificate. It was as if they had stuck a giant vacuum hose to our front door and everything we lived with every day was getting sucked out. When there was nothing left downstairs, the movers went up to the bedrooms.

In the hallway, they had stacked boxes labeled BOY ONE, BOY TWO, and BOY THREE. Dad was telling Gerry to throw away a stash of junk he kept in his top drawer. Then he saw me standing in the door. "Pitch the car magazines," he said.

"Do what?"

"Get rid of all those old magazines. There must be five years' worth. They're out of date anyway. Just pitch them."

"My magazine collection?"

"Yes. Do it now." He reached down and pulled a string

out of Gerry's hands. "It's just string," he said to Gerry, and Gerry howled.

I walked out.

"Ben," Dad called, but I didn't answer. I walked into Mom and Dad's room to sit on her chair. But her chair was gone. And their bed and their bureau. Their lamps, their pictures, their books and bookcase—all gone. Lined up against the wall was a stack of boxes. On each of them the movers had scrawled MOTHER. The empty room spun with light. I sat suddenly on the floor and held my head in my hands.

The rubber soles of Dad's boat shoes made a slapping sound on the bare floor.

His toe nudged my thigh. "I told you to toss the car magazines."

I looked up at him and saw his face creased with lines.

"What are you going to do with these boxes?" I asked. "Are you going to put them in the giveaway pile too?" I felt my voice go high. "Everything of Mom's?"

"Ben," he started.

I reached for the closest box and ripped the tape off.

Dad grabbed at my hand. "Ben," he hissed. "Stop it."

I shook him off and dug in the box. It was the stuff out of her top bureau drawer. An old wallet. A tape of Dylan and me playing rock star. A makeup case. A note to the tooth fairy. A little tiny bracelet that said BYRON. It was the only thing Mom had kept from the last baby, the one who had come too early.

And then a photograph Dad had taken of her last summer on the boat. I took out the picture.

He grabbed my wrist again. "Go take care of the magazines."

"Don't touch me," I told him, and jerked away. I held the picture up in his face. I shook it at him.

"This is mine," I said, and slipped it into my pocket. "It's mine, and you can't take it away."

CHAPTER SIX

ON *CHRYSALIS* I had a room of my own but nowhere to put the picture of Mom. Everywhere in the starboard quarter berth looked like somewhere that would get wet. I spread my five new car magazines under the mattress. The diesel engine book took up all the space on top of the hanging locker where I stowed my clothes. Finally I put Mom's picture inside the cover of the book. I knew no one else would ever open that book, and I liked having her there. I liked her hidden smile. She felt like my special secret, throbbing just inside the cover, like an engine in idle waiting to shift into gear.

The V-berth was now Dylan's private room. He had brought his clothes, his star books, and *The Chronicles of Narnia*. He had left his telescope behind because there was no room for that on a boat.

Boats don't have room for blocks or tricycles or Roller-blades either, so Gerry had brought only a few of his little cars and his markers. They all fit on the shelf above the starboard settee in the main cabin where he had decided to sleep. I had helped him pick out some of his favorite picture books. He spread them under the cushion of his bed.

Dad had the port quarter berth for his room. He had brought nothing with him except clothes and one book, a collection of poetry. He always said he could read a poem a hundred times and it would be new every time. I guessed he meant it.

But then in Key West, a new selection of books appeared. Now the books in our family room—the main cabin—were about sailing and the Bahamas, coral and marine life, snorkel-ing and spearfishing. Dad had clearly bought out the whole reference section of the bookstore. "No more poetry, please," he must have said. "Just give me the real stuff."

Of course he had to buy a lot of things besides books to get the boat ready to go. He bought a GPS, attached the antenna to the stern rail, and hooked up the display screen beside the nav table. Then he punched in the keys, and the screen told us exactly where we were. We hadn't needed that on the lake, but now he said we couldn't sail without it. He got a new outboard motor for the dinghy and a whole new set of life jackets. He outfitted the emergency pack with new flares and an EPIRB, a device that broadcast your position in an emergency so you had a chance to be rescued. After buying all that, he decided not to get new sails. We just hosed off the old ones with fresh water and bagged them properly when they were dry. The radio gave him a little trouble. It worked when the guy came to look at it and then stopped as soon as he left. But Dad fiddled with it and got it straight. He was glad not to have to buy a new one.

Dylan was working hard to learn navigation, especially sun shots. At noon, he sat with the sextant and measured the height and angle of the sun relative to the horizon. Then he did all kinds of mathematical calculations and slowly began to figure out that we were somewhere north of the equator. I figured he was a sort of junior Einstein to do that much, but he wanted to get better. He kept trying.

I was doing a different kind of hard work. Dad hauled me up the mast to mount a new anemometer for measuring wind speed. We trued the compass together. I replaced the lifelines. I broke down the engine and I scrubbed the hull. I think Dad would have even had me sand the teak and varnish it if he hadn't gotten impatient.

But soon he was ready to leave. We packed the boat with groceries and water. Dad drove the car to a used-car lot and walked home with a pocket full of cash. We took a long day sail to Marathon and tied up at the marina. That night Dad crawled into his bunk early. Gerry fell asleep in the cockpit lying next to me while Dylan and I stared up at a dark circle of starless sky surrounded by bright security lights.

"I don't want to go," I said to Dylan.

He didn't answer.

I rose up carefully on one elbow so I wouldn't wake Gerry.

Dylan was already asleep. How could he sleep?

It was just like the night after the movers had come when we had gone to bed on pallets we had made on the floor. That night Dylan's breath had settled easily into his usual deep sleep, while I had stayed wide awake, staring at the sticker stars on our ceiling and hearing every reverberating sound in the house. Downstairs, Dad's feet had thumped around in the empty rooms. Then the front door had opened and slammed shut. Dad had gone outside.

All of a sudden I had decided to leave.

I had crept downstairs carrying my duffel bag and shoes. Light from the streetlamps poured through the curtainless windows. I had headed toward the kitchen and the back door.

Then I had stopped.

Dad hadn't gone outside. He was standing in the kitchen leaning against the sink. He was bent slightly forward, pressing a large cloth to his face. I saw it was an apron.

"Dad?" I said.

He dragged the apron down over his face and turned to me. Then he held it up for me to see. "Christine's," he said. "The movers missed it. It was all the way in the back of the drawer."

Upstairs Gerry called out. "Mom?"

Dad looked down at the apron in his hands. "I wonder why they didn't see it."

Gerry's voice called louder. "Mom!"

"Dad," I said. "Gerry's calling."

"What?"

"Gerry's calling Mom—again."

"Mom!" Gerry's voice was going hysterical.

Dad looked toward the stairs then pressed the apron to his face again.

Gerry screamed.

I dropped my bag. I took the stairs two at a time. I lay down beside Gerry on the pallet. "Ben," he sobbed. I took the silky corner of Blankie and rubbed his cheek. He curved his body into mine. I felt him shuddering.

The next morning, we had thrown our duffel bags in the car and started driving.

Now I was lying next to Gerry again, this time in the cockpit of a boat called *Chrysalis*. Again in the morning we would leave. I looked at my sleeping brothers and then up, past the security lights, to the blank, black sky of night. I thought of the chart spread out on the navigation table down below and the long straight line Dad had drawn on it from Marathon to Bimini, the westernmost island of the Bahamas. In my mind, I looked at the line and it was like looking over the edge of a cliff and falling. Falling and falling and falling. Straight into the bottomless sea.

THE BAHAMAS

CHAPTER SEVEN

RIGHT UP UNTIL we threw off the lines in Marathon, I kept thinking Dad would change his mind. I kept thinking he would look at us all of a sudden and say, "Hey! What happened? Why are we here?" But it didn't happen that way. Just as he had said we would, we left Marathon in the early afternoon and sailed east, south of the Keys and out of sight of land. All around us was nothing but ocean, ocean, and more ocean. Florida was a few miles north on our port side. Cuba was a hundred miles to starboard. The high summer sun was slowly curving down toward Mexico behind us.

Ahead lay hundreds of islands, the Bahamas. We were pointing our boat toward Bimini, an island smaller than the lake at home. I sat in the cockpit, feeling the swells carry us rhythmically up and down and thinking maybe Bimini would be impossible to find even with Dad's fancy new navigation tools. I thought maybe I didn't really care, and if we were lucky, we'd keep right on sailing until we fell off the edge of the earth.

I shifted on my cushion and saw Dylan sitting on the port side, hanging his legs over the edge, trying to catch his bare toes in the foam that curled up the side of the hull.

"Toe bait," I said. "Sharks love it."

Dylan smiled. "The water looks beautiful this way. Come see."

"No thanks. I prefer to be miserable on a cushion."

Gerry climbed into the cockpit from down below. He was dragging Blankie with him. He moved carefully to sit down next to Dad. He curled his legs under him and balled Blankie up under his chin. It looked like a beard.

Dad didn't move. "What's our speed, Ben?" he asked.

I leaned forward to look at the speedometer. "Six knots."

Dad frowned. "We should be going faster in this wind."

"You're not steering high enough," I said.

"No." Dad shook his head. "I don't think that's it." He studied the sails a while longer. "We're heeled over too far," he said. "Got up too much sail. Why don't we raise the working jib."

I'd sailed with Dad on the lake enough to know that you don't argue. You don't say "Oh, let's not do that," or "Why don't you do it, Dad. I'm tired." The captain is always right, and on the boat Dad is always the captain. So when Dad said

"Why don't we raise the working jib," what he really meant was "Ben, raise the working jib."

I headed down below to get the other sail. When I came back up, Dylan was already on the foredeck getting ready to lower the genoa.

"Lower away," I shouted, and popped the halyard. The sail billowed down. Dylan gathered the folds and quickly un-hanked the sail, grabbing each metal clasp in a practiced motion and unhooking it from the forestay.

Dylan on boats was a mystery to me. He always seemed to be willing to go, and when he was on the boat, he always knew what to do and he always did his job well. But he never asked to take the tiller. He would take it if Dad told him to, and he could handle it just fine. But he never seemed to want to do it. He always seemed to be just along for the ride.

Now he was expertly stuffing the genoa into the sail bag and I was dragging the jib forward when Dad's voice stopped us.

"Wait," he said. "I forgot. This is shakedown time. Everybody learns everything. Gerry, you go hank on the sail. Ben, stand by to raise it when Gerry's done. Dylan, take the genoa down below and double-check our course."

It's true the lightest man is usually foredeck crew—at least in racing. But Gerry was more than light. He was little. He was barely five years old.

Dad pushed at him to get him moving. "Come on, buddy. Let's go. Leave Blankie here."

"Dad," he whispered. "I don't want to. It's too heavy."

"I'll do it," I said, and started forward.

"No, Ben. This is something Gerry can do. He's part of the crew. He needs to learn."

"Daddy—" Gerry started.

"Don't whine," Dad said. "Just go try."

Gerry crept to the foredeck on his hands and knees, then stood and grabbed the sail bag. It was heavy for him, but not too heavy. He managed to haul the sail out of the bag and stuff the bag down the forward hatch. Moving carefully, he ran his hand along the bottom edge of the sail, feeling for the tack. He snagged the huge grommet in the hook fixed on deck, then searched for the first hank.

I watched him struggling to open it. It was stiff. His fingers were small. He pulled it open and slipped the hank onto the forestay. He felt for the next one. Two. Three. The sail must have had fifteen hanks along its leading edge. Each one had to be hooked on before we could raise the sail. Four. Five.

"You're doing great, Gerry," Dad called. "But you need to hurry up. We need the jib to steady us." Dad was sitting back, his fingertips on the tiller, his eyes studying the head of the main. Dylan was down below at the chart table measuring distances.

Gerry balanced, concentrating on his job. His tongue stuck out and curled up toward his nose. He reached up to push his hair off his face. Then the boat hit a wave, and Gerry wasn't on the deck anymore.

I felt myself leaping to the bow and then reaching over

and grabbing his skinny wrist where he was clinging desperately to the base of the bow pulpit, his feet dragging in the water, too scared even to scream.

I hauled him up and held him between my knees as we sat breathless on the bow. I squeezed him there, and neither of us looked back to the cockpit where Dad was standing now and shouting at us, "What happened? What's going on?" Dylan stood in the companionway, quiet and watchful.

Gerry and I stayed still. I could feel waves rolling over me that weren't ocean. I could feel Gerry's skinny shoulders pressed warm between my arms.

"What's happening?" Dad shouted again.

"Gerry," I said. "One hand for the boat. Always. No matter what. One hand for the boat. Got it? Now go sit down. I'll finish this."

Gerry clung to the lifelines, moving so slowly that I had the sail hanked on and was raising it before he sat down in the companionway, frightened and chilled.

I didn't say anything to Dad as I winched the sail in close-hauled, leaning out to study the leading edge, bringing it in a little to relieve the luff. When the set suited me, I turned and looked at Dad.

"What happened?" Dad asked.

"Gerry fell overboard and I pulled him back on."

Dad's eyes flicked to the sail and then to the companionway, where Gerry sat with his back to us, Blankie draped over his shoulders like a shawl.

He didn't say anything. Not to Gerry or to me.

"Gerry fell overboard," I repeated.

"I heard you," he said. "Gerry, go get on some dry clothes. Ben, Dylan, we need to discuss proper man-overboard procedure."

Gerry disappeared down below and Dylan came up. I sat and watched Dad. I felt my pulse throbbing all the way to the ends of my fingers.

"Safety at sea," Dad said. "It's critical. We've got the equipment, but we need to know the procedures."

"Dad—" I said.

He held up his hand to silence me. "We should have gone over this in Key West," he continued. "Man overboard is fairly simple. In most cases you should throw over the life ring first. Then the man in the water swims to the ring while the boat turns around to pick him up." He stopped talking and looked at the compass.

"Dad." I held my teeth tight. "I guess you forgot. Planning this whole trip, I would have thought you'd remember, but I guess you didn't." I looked at Dad again. He was watching the sail. "Dad," I said, "Gerry can't swim. Remember?"

Something like a pain twisted across Dad's face. Maybe it was a memory.

Because the fact that Gerry couldn't swim was a family joke. Mom couldn't float. When we went to the pool, she loved to show off how she'd sink when she laid herself out to float on her back. "No moving," we yelled, and jumped around. Then we counted how many seconds it took for her to be underwater. She claimed her bones were made of rocks. If she worked at it, she could stay afloat, of course. But treading water exhausted her, and though she could swim, she hated it. She said she didn't know where Dylan and I came from. How had she spawned such fish, us both being swimmers practically at birth?

Then came Gerry. If he looked at water, he sank. Being on boats didn't change him. It just made Mom and Dad determined to teach him. When Dad tried, Gerry sank and cried, and Dad got mad. When Mom tried, he still sank, but Mom got sad. So at the pool Mom and Gerry splashed in the shallow end while the rest of us did backflips off the board and competed for who could hold his breath the longest. I always won.

Had Dad forgotten all that! Had he forgotten the morning of the accident, when Gerry had had his first official swimming lesson, and he had sunk? Had he forgotten that Gerry cried and Dad fumed? That Mom was mad because Dad was mad, and she decided the only way to calm everybody down was a treat. So she would make banana splits. Only we were out of ice cream. Had he forgotten how she slammed the door on her way out to the store and he had yelled, "You don't have to do this, you know," and she had hissed back, "*You* don't have to yell at a scared five-year-old!" Had he forgotten that the ice cream melted in the front seat while the ambulance—

Dad spoke quietly. "I didn't forget, Ben."

"Yes, you did," I said.

"I made a mistake. I should have told him to put on a life jacket."

"What about the ice cream? Did you forget the ice cream, too?"

"Ben, don't—"

"Everything!" I said. "You've forgotten everything, haven't you?"

I stood then and left him sitting in the cockpit. I went forward to stand in the bow pulpit. The wind blew in my face and the sail flowed out behind me like a single giant wing, like I was some kind of mutilated butterfly who could flap around a lot but who would never, ever fly.

CHAPTER EIGHT

I STAYED THERE IN the bow pulpit, watching the waves disappear into the blurring evening, until far in front of us the horizon was dark and behind us the sun had sunk into a bank of clouds. To our left, past Florida and then across a sweep of earth, across trees and mountains, across rivers and lakes, was home.

"Ben!" It was Dad's voice. "Dinner." As I stepped into the cockpit, he handed me a bowl. "Chili," he said.

I took the bowl and sat down. Nobody had anything to say, so we just listened to the autopilot. While I had been on the bow, Dad had set it up so no one would have to steer during the night. Now it was whining into our silence, adjusting the tiller slightly one way, then the other, holding a perfect course in the unchanging wind.

Dad set down his empty bowl. "Boys," he said, "this will be our first overnight passage. Everyone has a job to do. Gerry, your job is to sleep. The rest of us will have to take watches. Dylan, you'll take the first one—eight to midnight. I'll take midnight to four. Ben, I'll wake you at four for your turn. Every hour we need to record our speed and direction for navigation purposes. Ben, you'll be the one to spot Bimini, but it probably won't be until dawn. When we anchor, we'll all be on duty. We want to make sure we do it right." He paused and looked at me. "Aren't you hungry?"

I looked down at my bowl. I hadn't eaten anything. At home, I would be hungry. I would be just getting back from spending the day sailing alone or playing baseball and swimming in the lake with Andrew and the other guys. The little kids would be playing screaming tag games across the yards. The moms would be in the houses cooking dinner. By now those people, whoever they were, had moved into our house. They might find an old birthday candle on the back of a kitchen shelf. They might find an army man under the refrigerator or a baseball in the yard. They might open a drawer in Mom's bathroom and find a comb. They would throw it all away.

"No," I said, "I'm not hungry." I stood and tipped my chili into the sea.

"That was your dinner," Dad said, and snatched the bowl out of my hands. "There won't be anything else until tomorrow after we've anchored." He turned and went down below to clean up.

Gerry watched him disappear then curled up on his side

with his eyes closed. Since we had been on the boat, he hadn't had a nightmare, but he had developed a habit of curling up and sort of disappearing, like one of those roly-poly bugs that rolls into a ball when you touch them.

Dylan leaned back to look at the stars. "Look, Ben," he said. "There's the Milky Way." At home he had shown us the moons of Jupiter through his telescope and made a mobile of the planets to hang under the stick-on stars on our ceiling. He used to go outside and lie in the damp grass to watch the night sky. "The sky's so clear here," he said quietly, "you can see everything."

"I hate to break it to you, Einstein," I said, "but I don't really care that much about the stars."

He was quiet for a moment. "But they never change," he said. "And they've been there for so long."

I shrugged.

"I like stars," Gerry said suddenly, sitting up. "Tell me."

"Look," Dylan said. "That's the Little Dipper. See? The last star in its handle is the Pole Star, the only one that never moves. All the others spin around it. Now look down. That's the Big Dipper. It looks like the Little Dipper is pouring into the big one."

I followed his finger across the darkness. I thought maybe it would be good to look out into space and be blown away. I tried it. I looked up. I saw stars. I imagined space. But nothing happened. It was just night.

"Now look down from the last star on the Big Dipper's

handle," Dylan was telling Gerry. "That really bright one is called Arcturus. It's not even forty light-years away."

Dad climbed back up into the cockpit and stood, looking forward into the dark.

"What's a light-year?" Gerry asked.

"Six million million miles."

"Why is it miles if it's years?"

"It's too complicated, Gerry," I said. "You wouldn't understand."

"Because that's how far a ray of light can travel in one year," Dylan explained.

"Oh." Gerry was quiet a moment. "How many light-years is it to heaven?"

I felt heat wash over me and flashed a look at Dad.

He turned and spoke. "Ben, why don't you take Gerry and go on to bed."

"But I'm not sleepy."

"You have to be wide awake for your watch. You need to learn to sleep when you can. Go."

I started to say something, but then I stood and led Gerry down below. When I crawled into my tunnel, I could hear Dad and Dylan quietly talking above me and the water gurgling at my ear. Less than an inch of fiberglass stood between the ocean and me. Below me were fathoms of darkness and strange, goggle-eyed fish. Above me were the stars and the expanding universe. How was I supposed to go to sleep?

I punched the pillow and sweated. Gerry whimpered and

tossed. Eventually, Dad's and Dylan's voices stopped. Hours passed, and then Dylan moved quietly through the boat to bed. The rudder creaked in its housing. The boat's braces groaned. A line thumped against the cockpit floor. I felt I had just slipped into sleep when Dad shook my foot to wake me.

"Your turn," he said. "I'll show you how we've been tracking ourselves."

I barely heard Dad's explanation. I stood holding the companionway ladder and sorting through the facts. I am fifteen now. I used to be five. I am hungry. Mom is not here. Dad is talking. A red light is glowing on a map. I mean a chart. A chart. This is a boat. *Chrysalis.* A boat. We live on a boat.

"Ben!" Dad spoke sharply. "Wake up. Listen. It's your watch now."

I turned slowly to take my position at the helm.

"Ben," Dad snarled. He was tired. "Life jacket and safety harness. Always. When you're alone on deck at night, we'd never know if you fell off. You'd be left behind. We'd never find you."

"Doesn't sound so bad," I said, and shrugged into the hot, heavy gear. The safety harness was like a leash that moms put on two-year-olds at the mall, except you were hooked to a boat, not a mom. If I fell off it would be a pretty wild ride until somebody dragged me out.

As I sat down at the helm, I searched for the horizon I had been watching before dinner, but it had disappeared in the darkness. The stars were brilliant in the black sky, but I didn't remember any of their names. When Dad was finally quiet down below, I heard no sounds except the slap of the waves against the hull and the whine of the autopilot. There was nothing for me to do, and I felt sleep creeping over me again.

Suddenly a splash right beside the boat set my heart pounding. I sat up and looked, but if there had been a monster, I couldn't have seen it in the black night. Then I heard a cry. A voice called out. One hail from the darkness. Did it say "help"? Was it "ahoy"? Why not a second shout? I sat tense on the seat as my ears filled with the sound of my own blood. Then while I thought I was listening for the voice, I fell into a dream—running and falling, running and falling—until I shook myself awake, only to fall asleep once more. An hour later, when we were miles away from where we had been before, I heard the call again. I wanted to scream back, "Who are you? Where are you?" But there was only a single cry and then silence.

Then heat crackled through my body as an island appeared dead ahead. I could see its silhouette clearly—a gentle hill with two trees on top. We were much too close. A thin, white line divided it from the sea. That was a beach—or—I sat down. I held my head in my hands. It wasn't an island. It was a cloud. It wasn't a beach. It was the faint glow of the rising sun on the horizon just below the cloud.

When I lifted my head, the island was slowly changing. The thin, white line wasn't quite as thin, and the trees were slowly drifting away. Overhead, the stars were disappearing as the curve of our sails solidified to gray against the paling sky. Then far ahead of us, I saw the tiny ghost of another sailboat making its way to Bimini too.

My cheeks felt hollow, my skin dirty, and my stomach empty. I lay back on the cushions as the wind grew lighter and lighter. I looked out to the horizon, a place you never get to, and I closed my eyes against the hot pink ball of the new sun.

CHAPTER NINE

"WAKE UP!"

I sat up straight. Dad was standing in the companionway.

"I wasn't sleeping."

Dad jerked himself into the cockpit. He motioned me aside. "When did the wind die?"

I saw the sails hanging loose in the dead air. "Just now," I said.

"What's our speed been?"

"I'm not sure." I paused. "The wind's been getting lighter for a while."

"Since when?"

"Since the sun started coming up."

"How long ago was that?"

I didn't answer.

"Ben, how are we going to calculate where we are if we don't know how fast we've been going? Do you want to ram into a marker or run up on a reef?"

I snatched off the safety harness. "It hasn't been long."

"Time passes quickly when you're sleeping."

"I wasn't asleep." I threw the safety harness down.

"Pick it up," Dad said. "Put it where it belongs, then take down the sails. We'll have to motor the rest of the way."

"It's not my fault the wind died."

"Do what I said. Then keep a lookout for Bimini."

I followed his orders, then stomped to the bow, where I saw a dark streak growing on the horizon. Hours of sailing in the dark with no land in sight, and then there was an island. We'd found it after all.

"Bimini," I shouted to Dad, and he nodded.

I sat down forward of the mast, feeling the deck vibrate with the engine and watching the streak shifting shape every few minutes as we grew closer. When it had separated into two islands just like it was supposed to—North and South Bimini—Dylan and Gerry finally got up and joined me.

"I'm hungry," Gerry said as he sat down beside me.

"We have to wait," I said.

"Ben!" It was Dad's voice. "The engine."

I looked back and realized we weren't vibrating anymore and the world was quiet. The engine had stopped. I left Dylan and Gerry keeping watch and climbed down below. There was air in the fuel line. I didn't need the book to handle that one.

You just loosen the bleed screw and pump until you get fuel coming clean. It takes time, though. By the time I climbed out of the engine compartment, Gerry was eating a breakfast bar quietly in the cabin and Dad had had Dylan raise the sails again.

"The wind came back up," Dad said. "We can shut down the engine."

"But I just got it going."

"We don't need it. Shut it down."

I did what he said, then sat in the cockpit with my arms crossed over my chest. I clenched my jaw. A slow pound started in my head. The island developed trees and buildings and a beach. When Gerry climbed back out into the cockpit, Dad started yelling at us to help him spot the markers. We squeezed between two sandbars, heading north to the harbor while Dad kept quadruple-checking the depth and looking over to port, where the chart said the water was two feet deep and we could see the bottom shining up from the sandbar just under the waves.

A seaplane landed in the harbor just as we slid in. "Dylan!" Dad shouted. "Check the chart. We can't anchor in the run-way—or whatever you call it."

"Splashway?" I offered.

"Be quiet," he snapped.

"Fine." I stood up. "I'll go get something to eat."

"You can wait."

"I can't."

"When we're anchoring, we're all on duty. We'll eat when we're done."

"But Gerry—"

"Gerry is five."

I sat. I stared at this place, which wasn't at all what I had imagined. This was just a flat little island scattered with a collection of ragged buildings and old docks limping into the water. I turned my face into the hint of breeze. Gerry shifted as he rolled Blankie into a ball clutched under his chin. Dylan sat by the depth finder and called out changes. The sun got hotter. My stomach got hungrier. *Chrysalis* inched farther into the harbor. Then Dad said, "Here."

We knew how to anchor. We each had an assigned job. Gerry went below. Dylan watched the depth finder. I let out the anchor. Dad handled the engine and did the yelling. We all did our jobs pretty well that morning, especially Dad. He did some outstanding yelling on our first morning in the Bahamas.

When we finally got the anchor down to suit him, I headed straight to the galley to find something to eat. My hands were shaking when I ripped open a package of crackers. Then he was calling for me again.

I dragged myself halfway up the companionway ladder. The pain swelled in my head. Dad and Dylan had launched the dinghy and Dad was on his knees in it, trying to get the motor started.

"What do you want?"

"Come help me with this anchor."

"We already set the anchor," I said.

"We need another one at a hundred-and-eighty-degree angle to the first. The current runs through these harbors. We can't trust just one."

I dragged myself into the dinghy, still clutching the package of crackers. Dad motored us to a spot maybe 150 feet from where our first anchor had dug into the bottom. He dropped the second anchor overboard into the milky harbor water. It sank in a rustle of bubbles and hissing of line.

"Now," Dad said, "dive down and make sure it's secure."

"You think I'm just going to jump over and swim to the bottom right here in the middle of the harbor?"

"I know you are," Dad said. "I told you to." He reached out and took the crackers. "Go."

The rush of blood to my brain made me dizzy and hot. I couldn't look at Dad. We were about two swimming-pool lengths from shore where there was an old marina. A wooden dinghy drifted on a slime-browned towline next to a finger pier rotting into the water. The island looked no wider than the row of tall casuarina trees growing behind the peeling cinder-block building that must have been the marina office.

I sat for a second, then rolled backwards into the water. I held on to the anchor line and pulled myself down. The water was full of light all around me. The anchor was easy to reach where it lay in less than nine feet of water. I felt the flukes quickly where they dug into the sand and pushed myself straight back up.

Dad was looking at me as I broke the surface of the water. "Well?" he said.

"It's set."

"You actually touched it?"

"I touched it."

Dad grabbed the anchor line and tugged. The anchor held tight. He held out his hand to help me back on board. I looked at it for a second, then swam around to the other side of the dinghy and climbed on by myself.

I heard Dad drop his hand down on his thigh. I heard the silence while he looked at my back. I heard the motor start and the slap of waves against the dinghy bow. But I didn't turn around. I didn't want to see Dad. I couldn't stand to look at him anymore.

CHAPTER TEN

IT'S HARD TO live with someone you can't stand. Everything he does makes you mad—the way he drinks his coffee or the way every once in a while he takes a deep breath and then puffs it out through his lips. You can't watch him yawn or stretch or scratch. You can't stand to be close enough that you might touch.

And on the boat, we were always close. *Chrysalis* was just over thirty feet long. When we were all down below, only one person at a time could walk around without creating traffic jams. You had to claim your personal parking space. Dad either lay on his bunk reading poetry or sat at the navigation table working with charts. Dylan liked the port settee. Gerry and I went for our bunks. We stayed away from each other as much as we could. It was too tight. Too close. There was no place to go.

And it wasn't just the space that cramped you. It was also the work. Even normal things were hard to do. How do you cook dinner on a swinging stove or wash dishes in a sink the size of a mixing bowl? How do you get clean clothes when you're surrounded by seawater? Then there was the boat work. Every morning it was the same routine. When we woke up, Dad made us take the sheets off our beds, fold them, and stow them in our pillowcases. Next I had to haul up buckets of seawater so Dylan and Gerry could swab the decks while Dad cooked breakfast. After breakfast, Dylan and Gerry cleaned the galley while I took care of the head.

Once Dad was satisfied that everything was shipshape, we did whatever schoolwork he had set out for us and then started on his list of special chores. We spent hours rearranging the gear in the boat because every other day Dad came up with another brilliant idea about how to make it better. He made us check all the safety gear—the life jackets, the harnesses, even the man-overboard pole. He had us take everything out of the emergency pack and lay it out for inspection. We held our breath while he tested the EPIRB. You flip a switch, it beeps loudly for a minute, and then if it's working correctly it turns itself off. Otherwise, it starts broadcasting its exact GPS location, signaling the Coast Guard and the Bahamian Defense Force that the idiots on sailing vessel *Chrysalis* are in trouble and need rescue. I thought for sure the helicopters would appear any minute, but it turned itself off just like it was supposed to, and we weren't saved after all.

Every day it was exactly the same. Dad never let up.

After lunch and when the sun had eased off a bit, he let us do what we wanted. While he talked at the marina or studied charts or read books, we explored the harbor or the island and swam in the ocean.

When we explored the harbor, we took our snorkels and fishing gear. We thought we needed the masks to see what was on the bottom, but we were wrong. In the Bahamas the water was clear. From a distance it looked turquoise or royal blue, but when we were in it or looking straight down, it was as clear as a swimming pool. Everything was there for us to see. We might be skimming along in the dinghy when suddenly we would look down on a patch of turtle grass and several conch nestled against the sand. Or maybe we'd see an old engine sparkled with tiny fish. Or maybe the worst—a black plastic trash bag, flapping open and slowly losing its guts into the sea.

When we saw big fish, we tried to catch them. We used a pole or trolled a line the way we did on the lake. I told Gerry about when Dylan and I were very small and Dad let us put his trolling motor on my baby sailboat and go puttering around the cove. I got so excited about a fish that I forgot to steer, and we ran the boat right into the shore. Dad didn't even get mad. He just laughed at us and told Mom we should stick to sailing. When I told that story, Dylan laughed, but Gerry said he didn't believe me. "It's true," I said. "He really didn't get mad." Then I pretended I was going to ram the dinghy into a pier and Gerry pretended he wasn't scared.

A few times we explored the island. The houses were so

small. Cinder blocks—always with peeling paint. Trash and weeds in the yard. Through the windows, nothing but darkness and quiet. An occasional brilliant burst of flowers. Boogin—something. Mom would know the word.

Every day when we finished exploring, we walked across the narrow island to the ocean beaches. Dylan and I swam, but Gerry wouldn't even come in the water. Dylan and I put on our snorkels and masks and called to him, "Are you sure?" and he nodded. He sat on the beach, gathering shells and casuarina acorns and lining them up to make forts or armies or boats. Dylan and I waded into the water, watching our feet and the little puffs of sand we kicked up with each step. The schools of fish parted in front of us and the blue crabs scurried along the bottom. We laid ourselves out to float on the salty water and the warm swells lifted us toward the sun then eased us down again. When we came back to the beach, we helped Gerry build a sand castle. In the evening, when it was time to leave, Gerry stashed his acorns and shells near the roots of a tree.

We went back to the same spot every day. We liked it there. It was ours.

Then one day after we had finished up chores and schoolwork and lunch, Dad announced that this would be a short afternoon. "We'll all go in together. I have to shop," he said. "But we won't stay long. We need to get ready for tomorrow."

"What's tomorrow?" I asked.

"We're moving on," he said.

"Leaving Bimini?"

He nodded.

"But we like it here."

"It's time to go."

"Just like that?"

"Like what?"

"Like you just decide and we all have to go?"

"Well, you can't stay here alone," he said. "Come on. Everybody in the dinghy."

When the dinghy touched the dock, Dylan, Gerry, and I got out and left Dad to tie up by himself. We crossed the island without speaking. For a moment we all stood on the beach looking at the water.

"Gerry," I said, "the water is warm here. Not cold like the lake. And it's salty. You float better. You ought to try."

"No," he said, and scooped up his stash of acorns and shells.

"We can teach you," I said.

"I can't learn," he answered, and sat down beside the remains of yesterday's castle. The wind had softened all the edges. The water had collapsed one side. He started making repairs, and Dylan and I waded into the water.

Dylan put on his snorkel and mask and started puttering around looking at the bottom. I floated on my back and closed my eyes against the sun. I swam back and forth a few times and dove through some waves. Then I stood up, slung the water out of my hair, and waded back out. Gerry was not at his castle. I looked at the trees edging the beach and saw him sitting beside the tree where he stashed his acorns. He had pulled Blankie completely over his head.

I walked up to him and sat down. "I must have been swimming a long time," I said. "It's Halloween already and Gerry's a ghost."

He didn't move.

I started tickling up his spine. "Spider crawling up your back—"

He shook my fingers off. "Stop," he said, and hiccupped.

I pulled Blankie off his head. He was crying. "What's the matter?" I asked.

He didn't answer. He just looked at me then carefully arranged Blankie over his head once more.

I started to pull at the edge to slide it off again, but he grabbed it. "Stop," he said, so I stopped.

"Come on, buddy. Tell me what's wrong."

He drew in a deep breath and sat up straighter so Blankie seemed taller. "I don't want to go away again," he said.

I turned and saw Dylan just coming out of the water. He walked up to where Gerry and I were sitting. "Gerry doesn't want to leave," I said. Dylan nodded and sat down with us, the water dripping off the ends of his hair.

Then Dad came tromping through the trees to where we were sitting. "There you are," he said. "I wondered where you'd gone. Ready to head back?"

We didn't say anything.

"Gerry," Dad said. "What are you doing under Blankie?"

Gerry shrugged.

Dad patted him on the head. "Well, it works to keep off the sun. Come on, boys. Let's go." He pulled Blankie off Gerry's head and dropped it in his lap. As he was turning to walk back, he stopped and looked at Gerry again. "You're not wet," he said.

Gerry didn't answer.

"Don't you ever play in the water?"

Gerry shrugged again.

Dad looked at Gerry a moment, then sighed. "We'll have to change that," he said. "Soon." Then he turned and walked back through the trees.

Gerry took a long breath and looked at Dylan and me. "Did you know I can see you right through Blankie?" he asked. He rolled Blankie into a ball to hold at his stomach. "Don't tell Dad."

We walked back to the dinghy and climbed aboard. When I was shoving off the pier, my arm touched Dad's shoulder. I shuddered.

CHAPTER ELEVEN

AFTER WE LEFT Bimini, we went from place to place for several weeks, slowly sailing south. I wanted to tie up at a marina, but Dad said no, we were cruisers now and we didn't need a marina. I said I'd been on a boat for over a month and wanted a hot shower. He said I'd have to get used to it. I said I couldn't. He said shut up. And so on.

The truth was I couldn't get used to any of it—not being in the Bahamas, not living on a boat, not being so close together all the time. The Bahamas were nothing but a world of water with occasional dots of land so flat they were invisible from only a few miles away. The trees were twisted and small, and everything else that grew there stuck you. The sun glared, or it rained. There was no shade and no shadows, and living on a boat, we had no place to go. We were always together. We were never alone. It was just too different from home, where there were hills and trees and freshwater, where there were always other people and other rooms.

At home, I knew what the world would look like when I walked out. I knew what the weather would do, what people would say, what was going to happen in my own head. I would feel tired when I woke up. I would yell at Gerry for picking apart my models. I would get mad at Dylan for moving my car magazines to set up his telescope. When I rode my bike to the lake just before dark and listened to the crickets and watched the fireflies, I would be happy. I just knew that, and it felt good to know those things. But here I never knew from one day—or hour—to the next how things would look or what people would do or how I would feel. It was like constantly falling down. It was always a surprise. It wore me out.

I didn't tell Dad, of course. What was the use? He hadn't listened to me before. He wouldn't listen to me now. We just kept sailing from place to place to place until one day he said we'd stay longer at the next stop, Gun Cay. He said there were other things we needed to learn besides sailing.

We anchored just before lunch and then sat in the cockpit eating in silence until Gerry finally asked why this island was named Gun Cay. Dad had no idea. Dylan thought it was because of its shape. I said that made no sense because it was named before people flew over and saw its shape. Dad said they didn't have to fly over. Cartographers figured out the shapes of islands when they drew the maps. Dad and I got mad at each other and yelled. I started for the dinghy.

"Wait," Dad said. "We'll all go."

"Then I'll stay," I said.

"No," Dad said. "We'll all go. I need to learn to use the speargun. And there's a wreck here. You boys will like that."

So we loaded the dinghy and cast off. The waves were barely ripples on the shore. Dad tilted up the motor with perfect timing as we slid onto the beach. We heaved the dinghy high onto the sand, then walked closer to the wrecked boat.

It was a sad sight. The port side of the hull had been crushed against a coral head. The boat had slowly filled with water and now only the forward half still showed, a moldy gray lump rising above the waves. The mast was broken off with only a stub still intact. The rest must have sunk or washed away.

The sun was shining, but looking at the wreck made me feel cold.

"Okay," Dad said suddenly. "I'm going hunting." He took the dinghy out to stalk some fish and told the three of us to stay put on the beach.

Which we did, of course, since there was nowhere to go and no way to get there. At first we sat and watched Dad's head pop up occasionally while he practiced free diving just holding his gun. Before long, Gerry started dragging his fingers in the sand and digging a little hole. Dylan wandered off to the edge of the brush and started picking up dead leaves and sticks.

After a while, Dad started really trying to shoot a fish. I

could see him reeling in the line after a miss. A lot of misses, actually. I wondered what fish were still hanging around waiting to get shot.

Dylan made a boat from a coconut shell and sea-grape leaf and set it to float in Gerry's hole. The clouds passed over us, darkening the beach in spots and casting shadows on the distant sea. It was cooler, but only for a second.

Then Dad climbed in the dinghy and came back to us. "No luck," he muttered. "Couldn't really expect it on my first try."

"May I try?" I asked.

"Later," he said, and set the gun on a nearby log.

"I could do it," I said.

"Not today, Ben. Later."

He turned and walked away down the beach. I lifted the gun and aimed at a shell. "Pow," I said, then put it back on the log and sat down with Gerry and Dylan.

They had made a mess in the sand and had put together a pretty good little flotilla, but not a single ship would stay upright in the water. They were struggling to figure out how to fix them, and I had just picked up a boat to help when Dad walked up.

"Time for a family swim," he said. "Everybody in!" Then he looked at Gerry. "Everybody," he said.

"I don't want to, Daddy," Gerry said. He dug his hole deeper and refused to look at Dad.

"Gerry," Dad urged. "It's time you learned to swim. You can't sit out by yourself for a whole year."

"He said he doesn't want to," I said. "Come on. Let's make these boats float."

Dylan handed me a boat and Gerry jammed a stick sideways into the shore of his hole. "This is the dock," he said.

Dad stepped up and grabbed Gerry's arm, pulling him to stand. Gerry refused to walk. Dad bent, scooped Gerry up, and carried him into the water. Dylan and I were stuck there holding the coconut boats.

Then Dad dropped Gerry in, feetfirst, straight down.

Gerry's feet hit the bottom, his knees collapsed, and he went under for half a second before he popped back up screaming and grabbing on to Dad as if he wanted to climb him. "I stepped on something!"

Dad grabbed Gerry's chin and snapped his face up to look him in the eye, but Gerry's eyes were tight shut and he was hopping from one foot to the other, squealing and sobbing, water still running down his face.

"Don't be silly," Dad said. "Swim."

"But it wiggled, Daddy. It was alive."

"It was a fish. Do the dog paddle first."

"What kind of fish? A shark?" Gerry was peering into the water now, desperately ignoring Dad's command.

"A flounder, probably. Dog-paddle!"

"What kind of flounder?"

"I didn't see it. A peacock. Swim, Gerry. Put your head under and swim."

"Does it bite? Can you eat it?"

"Gerry. Shut up and go under."

"I can't."

"You can."

Dylan and I were standing now on the beach. Dylan was so close, I heard his quiet breathing. Dad really meant to make Gerry go under.

"Put your head under now," Dad said quietly.

"I can't."

Dad's hand, with the fingers spread out, covered the whole top of Gerry's head. His fingers almost reached from ear to ear. He pushed down, but Gerry wouldn't go under. He twisted out from under Dad's hand. He was screaming, but there was no one on the beach to hear him.

I realized then that I was standing there waiting for Mom to come—for her to step in and change everything. I was waiting, but she would never come.

Gerry was flailing out at Dad now, but Dad's grip on his arm was tight. "I said, 'Now!'" Dad said. Then he took Gerry by the shoulders and pushed him under the water.

I guess there are moments in your life when reality shifts and you enter some parallel universe where time is different and the things you do don't connect with who you were one second before. Just under the water I saw Gerry's blond hair waving and his hand stretched out and tense. I watched for what felt like hours. I felt myself go ice cold over my ears and down my spine. Then I raced into the water and jumped on Dad.

His shoulder rammed into my chest and my nose smacked

against his head. My arms wrapped around him, and I felt the rough elastic at the waist of his shorts and the rise of muscle on his chest as he let go of Gerry and turned his grasp toward me.

"Stop holding him down," I was screaming.

Dad threw me off and I fell backwards into the water. He stood there just looking at me as I struggled to stand. "What is wrong with you?" he said.

Dylan was leading Gerry to shore.

"Don't hold him down," I shouted, and turned toward shore.

"I was holding him up," Dad said to my back, but I pretended I couldn't hear him and slogged through the water to the beach.

When I caught up with Dylan and Gerry, Gerry was holding one of the coconut boats. I squatted down in front of Gerry and looked him in the eye. I couldn't tell if the water on his face was ocean or tears. "Which was scarier, Gerry—the fish or Dad?"

Gerry shrugged and looked off toward the trees.

"Next time," I said, "don't just stand there. Kill him. We'll eat him for supper."

"The fish?" Gerry asked.

I paused. "No," I said. "Dad." I looked up and there he was, standing at the edge of the water and watching us.

He was still my dad but now I hated him.

CHAPTER TWELVE

THREE DAYS LATER, we woke up to rain. While it rained, we sat in the cabin with everything closed tight, everybody knocking bones and sweating on each other. Trapped in the boat, the air got hotter and stuffier every minute. The portholes fogged over. The settee cushions got damp with the drips from the overhead hatches. Dad pondered charts at the chart table. Dylan and Gerry tried to see outside through the portholes. I crawled back into my tunnel and closed my eyes.

I planned my car, the one I intended to get as soon as I turned sixteen—the color, the interior, the paint trim, the factory extras, the things I would add. Then I took it for a drive. I drove down a long straight road. I propped one elbow in the open window. I draped one wrist over the steering wheel. I felt the wind in my hair. Then a long deep curve.

I held the accelerator steady. The wheels gripped the road. We leaned into it. And when the road straightened out again, I yelled and the wind sucked the sound away. I turned to the girl beside me and she smiled. I didn't wonder who she was or how she got there. I didn't wonder where I was going or where I was coming from. I just drove, the car's engine humming and the wind rushing in my ears. Like my blood.

"Wake up," Dad said. He shook my foot. "The rain's stopped."

I opened my eyes. "I wasn't sleeping," I said, and eased myself out of my bunk. The hatches were open. A slight breeze filled the cabin. Dylan and Dad were at the chart table. Gerry lay topsides in the cockpit, curled on his side with his eyes closed. I was halfway up the ladder to join him when Dad stopped me.

"Come look at the charts with us," he said.

I moved over and sat on the port settee. I picked up the logbook and opened it. Dad had already recorded the storm.

"This is the Great Bahama Bank," he was saying, his finger moving back and forth across the chart.

I looked at the date in the logbook. I'd already missed the first week of school. My name was already lined out in every roll book.

"Ben," Dad said. "I'm talking to you."

I looked up.

"I've decided," Dad said. "It's time to cross the Bank, and I think we're ready."

I put down the logbook. "Cross the Bank?" I said.

"Yes," Dad answered, spreading his fingers across the chart.

The Great Bahama Bank is a wide, flat underwater plateau. The Biminis and the Cat Cays where we had been sailing so far all lie along its western edge. The Berry Islands and Andros lie to the east. Between the two fringes of islands the ocean is shallow, twenty feet of water or less, with coral heads scattered around in certain areas.

"It's too shallow," I said.

When you first start out on a boat, being on the deep ocean makes you nervous. You're always imagining falling off the boat, and somehow the fact that the water is so deep makes it seem more dangerous. But after a while, you change. After a while, you realize that it's the boat that's keeping you out of the water, and you want the boat to be safe. Then you get nervous when you can see the sand sliding by under your keel.

"It's plenty deep," Dad said. "*Chrysalis* only draws five and a half feet. She could sail in six feet of water if she had to. Twenty will be more than enough."

"I still don't like it."

"I'm not asking you to like it. People cross the Bank all the time."

"But why do *we* have to cross the Bank?"

"To get to the rest of the Bahamas," Dad answered.

"You said we'd stay here awhile. We like it here."

"I changed my mind. The weather's good for crossing. We'll stay longer at the next place. We'll sail tomorrow night."

"At night!" I said. "We have to do another night passage?"

"We can't make it all the way across in one day, and the tide is right tomorrow night."

"I don't want to sail all night."

"It's just one night."

"I don't want—"

Dad suddenly slapped the chart with both hands. "I am the captain. I have decided. We're leaving tomorrow night."

"I'm not going," I said quietly, and turned to climb the companionway ladder.

Dad's hand flashed out and grabbed my arm. "Yes, you are," he said.

"No, I'm not."

"Ben!" He shook my arm. "You're turning this trip into a nightmare."

"*Turning* it into a nightmare?" I tried to pull away. "It was a nightmare to start with. We didn't want—"

"Shut up."

"Make me."

He dropped my arm and looked at me. "Just leave," he said quietly, turning away. "Just go. Get out."

I climbed into the cockpit where Gerry was now sitting up, his eyes big and Blankie pressed against his mouth. I stepped to the edge of the boat.

"What are you doing, Ben?" he asked.

"Leaving," I said, and dove into the water.

I swam underwater as far as my breath would take me, then surfaced and turned back to look at the boat. They were all standing in a row along the side looking at me.

"Ben!" Dad screamed. "Get back on the boat!"

I turned and swam toward the island, but my stroke felt weak and wobbly.

"James Benjamin Byron," he yelled. "Come back here now."

I paused, treaded water, and turned again to look at him.

"Go to hell," I screamed. "Go to hell—all of you!"

I turned again and swam toward shore. This time my stroke was stronger and my breathing much, much easier.

CHAPTER THIRTEEN

WHEN MY FEET touched bottom, I stood and waded to shore without looking behind me. Then I immediately turned left and started walking south. If they were watching, they would see that I didn't look back, that I knew where I was going, that I had a plan.

The plan was simple. Dad had said I was ruining the trip. He didn't want me there. He had told me to leave. Well then, I would just stay on Gun Cay. Another sailboat would come. I would bum a ride to a nearby town. I would lie about my age, and in a day or two I'd have a job somewhere and I'd be gone for good. He would never see me again.

After the storm, the wind was light and the surf was still. Seagulls squawked and scattered as I approached, but everything else was quiet. Even *Chrysalis*. They weren't calling out to me. They had not launched the dinghy to come get me.

It was almost noon already, the sun was hot, and I didn't have a hat. Still I didn't slow down. I kept walking until the beach curved. When I finally paused to look back, *Chrysalis* was out of sight. I stopped. I could hear the casuarinas quietly sweeping the breeze with their long blue-green needles. I could hear the surf roll gently in, fold over, and slip away. I had not been completely alone since we left home.

I looked out at the ocean. That turquoise water. That pale sand. That emptiness. I wondered if a person could ever get used to it.

I waded into the perfectly clear water. I swam out and floated, facedown, all alone in the sea.

Looking down was like looking through a clarifying lens. The bottom was in sharper focus than the sand at my feet when I walked on the beach. I drifted over the waving grass and dirty gray shells, over fish that swam into my shadow then turned in a split second and swam away.

I turned over and lay spread-eagled on my back on top of the waves. The sun warmed my chest and face. My ears filled with the sound of the water. I opened my eyes on the sky and floated effortlessly over the sea. I wanted to feel clean and empty, like an open dinghy drifting free. I wanted to be blank and invisible.

But I was not. I was a boy floating in the ocean getting sunburned and hungry.

I wondered if Dad would leave without me. I wondered if Dylan and Gerry would let him.

Suddenly the sea felt cold even though the sun was hot. I swam back to shore and stretched out on my stomach on the sand. I lay resting my forehead on my crossed forearms, my nose a quarter inch from the sand. It was dark in the cave my arms made.

I was tired. I was hungry. I hadn't spoken a word since my last words to them.

I could still feel the way my mouth had moved as I shouted. I could still see the way they had stood there along the deck of the boat as the words hit them.

I rolled over on my back again and lay faceup to the sun. I knew what Mom would say. "That's not worthy of you, Ben," she would say. "You're better than that."

But she was wrong. I was not better than that. I was clotted and swollen. I was dirty and crusted. And Dad. Dad was not the person she thought he was, either.

After a while on the beach, I went up to the trees and sat in the shade. I was thirsty and getting hungrier. I looked around for berries or nuts. I thought of trying to find a spring, but I couldn't go far into the trees with no shoes or shirt. Empty coconut hulls lay on the beach, but none of the palms had coconuts in them. And I couldn't have climbed a palm tree anyway without ripping my skin to shreds. I wondered how long I would have to wait for another sailboat. I wondered how people had ever managed to live on these islands.

When evening came, the air cooled and a slight cloud cover drifted across the stars. What would Dylan do tonight without stars to watch? I wondered if it was lonely for Dylan up there among the stars? Did he like it empty? Was all that emptiness like the good part of being dead? The part where you aren't angry anymore, where you never feel scared?

In the dark, I walked slowly back up the beach until *Chrysalis* came into view. I sat on a log at the brush line so they couldn't see me. I could hear muffled voices. Light shone out the cabin windows and reflected on the water. Someone came on deck and went forward. I knew it was Dad checking the anchor. Someone else joined him. Dylan, I was sure. They stood together on the bow for a moment. Then I saw white flashing in the cockpit and knew it was Blankie. "Dad," Gerry called. "Where are you?" The pair at the bow returned to the cockpit, and in a moment all the lights were gone. The boat was a shadow floating on the waves and I was alone on the beach.

For my birthday last year, Mom had asked me if I wanted a party. I told her no. I told her I wanted to take the boat out, just Andrew and me, and camp out at one of the coves on the lake. She said she would make a basket of food. Dad made sure I knew how to operate the radio. In the end, I didn't invite Andrew. I decided I wanted to go by myself. Mom was worried, but Dad said I was old enough to go alone.

I left late in the afternoon and sailed as far as I could before evening came. I anchored in a cove where a stream came down out of the hills and made a marshy mess in one corner. Across the cove from the stream lay a wide pebble beach littered with dried sticks and small logs. Beyond the beach, the forest floor was already soft with newly fallen leaves.

I inflated an air mattress and floated my sleeping bag, the food basket, and some dry clothes to shore. The weather was clear, so I didn't bother with a tent. After I changed, I hiked around the edge of the woods until dark, then built a fire on the beach and roasted my hot dogs and marshmallows. I sang "Happy Birthday" to myself, then lay back on my sleeping bag and looked up toward the sky.

Though I could remember it later, at the time I didn't really see the sky or the black tips of the trees ringing the cove. I didn't hear the hoot owls or the scurrying creatures in the leaves. I didn't feel the pebbles under me or the dampness of the dew as it settled in my hair.

What I felt that night, lying there alone and faceup to the sky, was open and cleaned out and strong. I felt invisible and perfect.

I did not want to move and I did not want to sleep.

When I woke in the morning, I sailed slowly back to the dock and bicycled home. My life was good. I wanted to keep it just the way it was. School and friends, parents and brothers, my bike and the boat, and sometimes just me—just me, a wide sky, and an open space of time. It seemed like something a person could always have. It seemed like something you could depend on, something you could trust.

I was wrong.

I watched the dark silhouette of *Chrysalis* for a long time. Then I waded into the black ocean and stroked gently into the dark. When I reached the boat, I pulled myself into the empty dinghy hanging just astern. I hauled the dinghy hand over hand to the boat and climbed into the cockpit. When I stepped on deck, the fiberglass felt smooth and cool after the acorns and shells on the beach.

Then I saw Gerry. He was sitting on the cockpit bench, his back resting against the cabin. He had been watching me.

I crossed the cockpit slowly and knelt quietly beside him. His eyes glittered at me like stars in the night.

"That was mean," he said. "What you said."

"I know."

"When you're mean like that, it scares me."

I didn't answer.

"Don't go away again."

"I won't."

"Promise?"

"Promise."

He stood, quietly climbed down the ladder, and laid himself in his berth, carefully touching a corner of Blankie to his nose.

I looked back at the beach and then up to where the mast rose black against the dark sky. I was surprised that Dad had forgotten to turn on the anchor light. I flipped the switch, then stood in the companionway to check. Yes. There it was—tiny and white at the top of the mast, swaying gently in the dark, the only light in the cloudy sky.

I was glad I had turned it on.

CHAPTER FOURTEEN

I DECIDED TO CALL a truce with Dad. I didn't say that
to him, of course. I just said as little to him as I could. The
next day when we mumbled good morning to each other, he
didn't ask why I had come back. I didn't say. After breakfast,
when he said we'd start across the Bank that afternoon, I
was quiet, even when he looked at me and waited for me to
speak. After he went topsides to study the clouds, I pulled
out a book. If we were going to go, I decided to figure out
where it was we were going.

Dad was right. No matter where we went from Gun Cay,
we had to cross the Bank. It was shallow, but I wasn't really
afraid. And the night would be long, but I could manage it.
Thinking about it twenty-four hours later, I couldn't really remember why I had jumped overboard and spent the whole day
alone on the beach.

So I was quiet as we raised the anchor and turned the bow east, farther and farther from home. The wind was light, barely filling the sails. We glided slowly through the water like a ghost, but at least we moved. Gerry and I went below to sleep right after dinner. At some point the engine came on inches away from my head. The noise shocked me out of sleep, but I was tired. I put the pillow over my head and slept on.

When I took the helm at four o'clock, the engine was still going. I poured myself a cup of hot, sweet coffee and snapped into my safety harness. Dad had left the main up to steady us and to catch what little breeze we might find. I double-checked the course, the autopilot, the rpms, the knots. I heard Dad snoring before I was comfortable in the cockpit.

Then the night grew large. It curved up over me out of the ocean. I saw strange lights. I heard voices cry out. I found myself standing quickly and peering into the invisible ocean around me. I knew it was all phantoms in my head, but it was hard to believe that something so real was just something my mind invented.

I tried Dylan's trick again and stared at the sky. Dylan was wrong. The stars did change. The Milky Way wasn't even in the same place it had been when I went to bed. Arcturus was gone and Orion was advancing from the east, his shield pointed west and the three bright stars of his belt clearly visible. Then they all started to fade.

The sky slowly separated from the ocean and the sea monsters resolved into clouds. The light I was supposed to watch for still hadn't appeared. We didn't seem to be making enough speed through the water for the rpms we were putting out. I didn't look forward to a day of creeping across a flat sea with the engine shaking the boat and covering everything with the nauseating smell of diesel fumes.

At six o'clock Dad crawled up out of the companionway looking old. He hadn't shaved since Key West and his beard had come in scruffy and thin. When he was young, his hair had been blond, but now it was dark, and the gray showed more and more as it got longer.

"How's it been?" he asked. His voice was normal—tired, but normal. I thought maybe he'd forgotten to be angry this morning.

"Good," I said. "No adventures."

He nodded. "Coffee?"

"Sure."

He disappeared down below and I sat with my heart pounding, waiting.

He came back up and handed me a cup. I tasted it. He'd put in the sugar I like. I could hardly drink it. This was my old dad come back, just like that. Right up the companionway into the new morning.

He sat down and sipped at his cup. I remembered that from home. The way he held the cup in two hands and brought it to his face like a bowl. He sipped. He paused. He sipped. Three times. Then he lowered the cup into his lap, took in a deep breath, and arched his back into a slow stretch.

"Seen the light yet?" he asked.

"No. Nothing yet."

"Nothing?" The edge of his voice sharpened and I felt something spinning away from me. Something it would have felt good to remember. It was gone and the small of my back felt tired and tight.

"No. Nothing yet."

"You've held your course?" The lines were starting back into his forehead.

"Yes," I said. "I've held my course."

"Are you sure? Did you fall asleep? You got tired. We're off course. I know it. Go get Dylan up. We'll put him on the bow pulpit to watch." Dad was spilling his coffee as he twisted around, looking for coral heads.

"Dad," I said, trying to keep my voice level. "I've held my course. I did not fall asleep. Something's not right with the engine."

"But it's been running all this time. I heard it."

"Yes, but we're not getting enough power from it. There's a current through here with the tide and all, but—Well, I think something must be caught on the prop."

Dad nodded. I saw his jaw working. "Okay. Someone has to jump in and look. Go get on your swimsuit."

Of course. Just like the anchor in Bimini. While Dad turned off the engine, I went down below to put on my swimsuit. Gerry was still sleeping in his ball. Dylan lay with one arm thrown up, circling his head. I left them and found Dad securing a line on a cleat off the back of the boat.

"You can't wear a life jacket because you couldn't get under the boat that way. But I'll float the life ring behind the boat so you'll have something to grab if you need it."

I stood on the stern and looked over. The sun was up high now. Already the air was getting hot. I could see straight down. The bottom was clearly visible. Even the ripples in the sand showed. We drifted past a patch of brown turtle grass, and a fish flashed in a glint of light near the rudder. I waited a moment, the night and the sleeplessness crushing my consciousness to a tiny spot of dread at going over into the ocean with no land in sight. Then I jumped.

The water was cool and clean. I came quickly to the surface and saw the boat already twelve feet away from me. I poured my energy into my strongest crawl, dragging myself through the water to the boat. Still it crept forward. I had closed the distance by only two feet. I was spent. I grabbed the line and let it slip between my fingers until I had the life ring in my grip. Dad was calling to me as I wiped the water out of my eyes.

"What's wrong?"

"I can't catch up. I can't swim that fast."

Dylan came up behind Dad. The mainsail hung lifeless on the mast, but they moved to take it down too. The halyard whirred, the sail flapped, and I rode on the life ring, feeling the cool, clear water around me and watching the bottom slip by. A great wad of seaweed floated by. Sargassum. Yellow-brown and knobby. It headed straight for me. I stuck out my arm and pushed it away. It floated stupidly toward the horizon.

I pulled myself hand over hand along the trailing line back to the boat's stern.

Dylan was leaning over, watching the water run by the boat. "I think we've stopped now, Ben," he said.

I dove again. Under water was completely silent except for the trailing line slapping the surface and the *whushing* water moving around *Chrysalis*. I could see perfectly. There was the rudder, newly slimed since Dad had bought her with a clean bottom, and there was the prop with a huge ball of sargassum wrapped round and round it, trailing back toward the rudder. Then I was out of breath. I popped up to the surface.

"Seaweed," I gasped, and dove under again. This time I swam immediately for the prop with my hand outstretched. I touched the seaweed and grabbed. A handful pulled away from the blades. I was out of air. I surfaced. I gasped. I dove. I pulled. Five times. Down under the belly of the boat, a grab, and then up, gasping for air. Finally I grabbed the right strand and the seaweed pulled away completely. The prop was free.

As I surfaced, I could feel my heart thudding in my ears. I eased up out of the water like a turtle poking up its head. I floated for just one second and then turned to Dad and Dylan. The boat was already twenty feet away. The wind on the mere sides of the boat, the tiny wisp of wind we were trying to catch in our sails, was moving the boat that fast. For a flash I imagined the boat sailing away and leaving me there, floating on the Great Bahama Bank. I could see the bottom, but it was too deep for me to stand on. Coral heads were somewhere, but they were invisible from here. Boats would sail by, but they wouldn't see me. At night, they would assume my cries were the mysterious cries of the night sea. I would float and float and float. No one would ever find me.

I shivered and grabbed the last foot of the line as it slid by. Dad reached out his hand to help me back on the boat, and I took it. He handed me a towel. "You called that one right," he said, and squeezed my shoulder. When he started ordering us around again, I looked over the side and watched the water. His instructions, his complaints, his criticisms—I let them all go past me. Looking in the water, I felt sad for Dad.

And a little sad for us too, I guess.

The tiny breeze dried the salt water on my skin to a sticky film. Dylan handed me another cup of coffee. Twenty minutes later, Gerry spotted the light. We took a fix on it. When it was due north, we turned south, heading for Joulters Cay on our way to Andros.

The wind picked up. We turned off the engine and raised the sails. I stood at the bow, balanced against the lift and fall of the waves, watching the flat, moving disk of ocean surrounding us. The water creamed under the bow and the boat bent into the taut pull of the wind across the curving sails.

Then I was glad—glad that we were picking our way into Joulters Cay after a long night crossing the Bank. Glad that we could see the coral heads and that the chart was clear about where the shallows were. Glad as we curved around to the southern tip of the island and dropped our anchor into the clear, bright water that filled this new world around us.

CHAPTER FIFTEEN

WHEN WE FINISHED anchoring at Joulters Cay that morning, I remembered that I had been up since four A.M. and climbed into my bunk to nap. Dad was under the boat, checking out the prop. Dylan was stationed at the rail to hand him tools as he needed them. Gerry was in the cockpit under the shade of the bimini. He had added acorns and coconut hulls to his car collection. The hulls were buildings. The acorns were bombs. I could hear the acorns hitting the cockpit seat right over my head and dropping to the floor. Gerry's voice told some story. Then Dad yelled for something and Dylan's feet pounded over my head.

It was impossible to sleep.

I turned and looked out the tiny porthole in my bunk. All I could see was the surface of the water. Then Dad's head popped up in the middle of my view. He spat out his snorkel and called for Dylan again.

"I need a knife," he yelled.

I heard Dylan's feet and saw his shadow fall over Dad.

"Don't just drop it to me," Dad said. "Tie a line on it."

Dylan was busy and then Dad swam toward the side of the boat and out of my sight. "A little more seaweed," I heard him gasp. "Won't pull off."

Another splash and he was back under the boat. I heard bumps against the hull as he swam toward the prop.

Everything went quiet. Gerry had stopped bombing his cars. Dylan was waiting for Dad to surface again. In a split second I was asleep.

It was a good sleep. Like drifting off lying on the couch on a spring afternoon when birds are in the trees and someone is mowing his lawn. But the lawn mower stopped. I opened my eyes. I wasn't on the sofa. I heard shouting and bumping. The water outside the window glittered and then I heard Dylan calling me.

"Ben!" he was shouting. "Come up here! Hurry!"

I looked up stupidly. Gerry appeared at my feet. "Hurry, Ben," he said, and raced away. "He's coming," he yelled as I crawled out and stumbled on deck.

Dylan was crouched at the rail, holding on to the lifelines with one hand and to something far over the boat's side with his other hand. The thing was Dad. Dad was gripping Dylan's arm with his left hand and holding his right hand pressed in a fist against his chest. Blood streamed from his hand down his chest and pooled in the water.

"Bad cut," he said through white lips. "I can't pull myself onto the boat."

I reached over and grabbed Dad's arm with Dylan. We pulled together, but it was no use. We couldn't lift Dad's weight.

"Hold up your other arm," I said. Dad lifted his right arm and blood pumped out of his hand and down his arm. I grabbed his arm. It was slick. Dylan and I pulled again, but Dad was still too much for us.

"The dinghy," Dad said.

"And life ring," I said to Gerry. He threw it overboard and Dad grabbed it as Dylan and I untied the dinghy from where it was stowed over the forward hatch. As we flipped it right side up, the emergency pack fell out. I shoved it toward Gerry, who held on to it while Dylan and I slid the dinghy into the water. Dylan held the towline while I lowered myself into the dinghy and turned its side toward Dad.

Dad grabbed it with his left hand and then lifted his right arm over the gunwale so the blood was falling into the dinghy. I grabbed under his right shoulder, and he pulled with his left arm. He kicked a few times, the dinghy rocked, and then he scraped on his belly over the side and into the floor of the dinghy.

Lying on his back, he held up his hand. "Pressure," he said. I grabbed his hand and saw that the cuts sliced evenly across the inside of the second knuckle of all four fingers and through the middle of his palm. It was impossible to tell how deep they were. I pressed my hand against his and blood oozed between my fingers.

Dylan and Gerry stood on *Chrysalis*, looking into the water. I followed their gaze. Sharks. Not very big, but sharks. Three of them.

I turned and looked at Dad. Tears were sliding from under his closed eyes.

"Your hand hurts," I said.

He shook his head. Then he spread his left hand across his chest and turned his face away. His lips barely moved. "I'm sorry," he whispered.

I held his hand and squeezed.

That night Dylan and I sat out under the stars. I kept replaying in my mind Dad's bleeding fist clutched against his chest and the warm, slick feel of the blood when I grabbed his arm to pull him on board.

After we had gotten him on board, he had slowly opened his hand and begun to give us instructions—pressure, cloths, boiling water, antiseptic. We all worked, even Gerry, for an hour to clean and bandage his hand, to get everyone into blood-free clothes, and to clean the boats.

He told us what had happened. He had untied the knife from the line and kicked his way under the boat. He was hold-ing a prop blade with his left hand and cutting at a tightly wound piece of sargassum with the knife in his right hand. Suddenly the seaweed split away and he dropped the knife. It balanced momentarily on the prop shaft. He grabbed it just as it slipped free. When his hand closed, it closed around the blade.

At lunchtime Dad had insisted that we eat. He sat in the cockpit fumbling with a sandwich, trying to hold it together with his left hand. Finally he let me cut it into four pieces for him. Then he let me pop the top of his soda.

"People manage with one hand all the time," he complained, and then pushed the sandwich away. "I'm not hungry," he said.

"Why don't you lie down?" I asked.

"I'm not tired," he snapped.

"When I cut my foot," Gerry said quietly, "Mom made me go to bed. She said getting hurt makes people tired."

Dad drew in a deep breath. He paused, then sat back and exhaled.

"Okay," he said. "I'll rest. Ben, if anything—*anything*—happens, wake me."

I nodded.

Dad slept all afternoon. When he got up, we changed his bandage because it was bloody. He wasn't very hungry for dinner but sat quietly in the cockpit while we ate. Before long, Gerry went to bed, and then Dad, Dylan, and I were sitting in the dark.

"Don't you think we ought to take you to a doctor?" I said.

"No," he answered.

"You're hurt bad. You need a doctor."

"I'll be fine."

"Maybe you need stitches."

"They're not that deep."

"What if they get infected?"

"I am not going to a doctor." He stood, holding his hand against his chest, and carefully negotiated the companionway ladder.

Dylan and I were still as we listened to him climb into his bunk. Then we moved to the foredeck and lay down side by side. I expected Dylan to start a star lecture, but he was silent. Eventually I heard him breathing deeply. "You asleep?" I whispered.

"No," he said quickly.

I propped myself up on one elbow and looked down at him. In the starlight I could see his cheeks were wet. "You're crying," I said.

He didn't answer. I lay back down. His breathing slowly grew quieter.

"Is that the Pleiades?" I asked. "Just rising over there?"

"Yes," he answered, but said no more.

"I never saw so much blood," I offered after a while.

"Me neither."

"Those sharks. They came from nowhere. They seem so stupid and then—"

"They're not stupid about blood."

We lay in silence again.

"Right after Dad got in the dinghy," I said, "tears were coming out of his eyes. I asked him if his hand hurt. He shook his head. Then he said he was sorry."

"For what?"

"He didn't say."

After a moment I went on. "I haven't seen him cry since we got on the boat."

"Except once," Dylan said.

"When?"

"The other day when you stayed on the island."

I held my hands in tight fists. "You just think he cried," I said.

"No," Dylan said. "I watched him. He sat at the chart table after you left. At first he just stared. Then he covered his face with his hands and shook."

"Then he stopped."

"No. Then Gerry patted him on the shoulder and he took Gerry in his lap and then he stopped."

I took a deep breath, flexed my fingers, and slowly exhaled. "What did you do?"

"I got out the Bahamas book and started reading about the Great Bahama Bank."

I turned to look at him. "You weren't upset with me?"

"I knew you'd come back," he said.

"How could you know that?"

"You're our brother," he said. "You'd never leave us."

CHAPTER SIXTEEN

DYLAN MADE THE best doctor. He was good at changing Dad's bandage. Gerry was good at handing Dylan the things he needed. I was good at getting out of the way.

They sat in the cockpit, and Dylan slowly unwound the bandage from Dad's hand. Then Dad held his hand out over the edge of the boat while Dylan washed it and poured antiseptic over it. Dad jumped and hissed every time the medicine hit his hand. Then Dylan rewrapped the hand in clean bandages and took the old ones to wash and boil.

Dad said we would stay until he felt stronger. For the first few days, he spent most of the time lying in the cockpit and wouldn't let us leave the boat. Gerry wanted to know if the sharks were still there. Dad said no, but he wouldn't let us swim anyway. Then he completely changed his mind and decided I had to learn to use the speargun. Fresh fish would be good for us, and our supplies would last longer. He made Gerry watch a fishing line off the stern and sent Dylan and me in the dinghy with the speargun. It took me several times, but I finally brought back a grouper. Dad stood over me while I cleaned it to make sure I did it right. He told me how to cook it, and we had a fish feast that night.

By the second week, Dad was much better and Dylan and I started taking the dinghy out just to explore, sometimes with Gerry. On the far side of Joulters Cay was a huge flat that lay bare at low tide. We walked out and felt we were walking into the middle of the ocean. We found conch hiding in patches of turtle grass and brought them back to the boat. Dylan wanted to eat them the way the Bahamians do, but we couldn't figure out how to get the meat out of the shell. In the end, we just put them back in the water.

When we got back to *Chrysalis*, Dad always had something he wanted me to do that he couldn't manage with one hand. Once he had all the spare lines out and was trying to coil them again. It took me an hour to get them straightened out. Another time he was trying to inspect the emergency pack while we were all gone and dropped it overboard. He had pinned it up against the side of the boat with the boat hook, but he couldn't lean over far enough to grab it. I don't know how long he had stood like that waiting for us to get back, but I know he was angry when we returned. I always did what he asked and didn't say anything. We would have just ended up fighting.

By the third week, he was ready to swim, so we all took the dinghy to the beach. Dylan, Gerry, and I started a hole in the sand while Dad swam back and forth, looking as strong as he had ever been. After a while he called to me, "Ben. I'll try the gun."

I waded out and handed it to him. He held it in his left hand and carefully fitted his right hand around the handle. He winced as his forefinger reached for the trigger.

"No," he said. "Not yet."

I took it back and turned toward the beach.

"It's time to leave," he said. "Don't you think?"

I stopped and looked back at him. "Leave?"

"Head south. To Andros."

"Andros?"

"I'm rested now. We're running low on water and food. We've been here three weeks. It's time to go, don't you think?"

"Okay," I said.

"That's decided then," he said, and lay back in the water to float.

At Andros, we tied up at Morgan's Bluff just long enough to fill our cupboards with groceries and our tanks with gas and water. Then we anchored and went to look at the reef. The eastern side of Andros is edged with a shallow plateau that is only a few hundred yards wide on the northern end of the island but is a few miles wide farther south. The entire edge of the plateau is crusted with a continuous reef covered by only six feet of water. Just past the reef, the bottom plunges down a cliff to a depth of over eight thousand feet. The different kinds of coral on the cliff are so thick, they fight one another for space. Every shape, every color, every texture is laid out there in the water below you—and it's all alive.

Every day for a week, we dinghied out to the reef and swam. Though Dad's hand was getting better and better, he still couldn't handle the speargun, so I kept my job as chief hunter. Dylan positively identified a blacktip shark and started making a list of all the coral we had seen. And Gerry finally got tired of spending all his time alone in the dinghy. He didn't actually learn to swim, but he started getting in the water in a life jacket. At first he just held on to the dinghy gunwale to learn what the life jacket felt like. Then he held on to a short line and kicked a little bit. It wasn't really swimming, but it was as close as Gerry had ever gotten.

After a week, we hauled up the anchor and sailed down the eastern side of Andros, ducking into each of the little harbors along the way to stay for a few days before heading south again. We had to learn to sail inside the reef. Gerry handled the depth finder, shouting out the numbers every time they changed. Dylan was an expert with the charts, matching up what he saw in real life with the numbers and lines on the paper. I stood on the bow and watched the sea. Before long, I could tell the depth by color before Gerry even read off the numbers.

By the time we pulled up at Pigeon Cay before making

the final run into Fresh Creek, we had developed a whole new afternoon routine. After anchoring, Dad and Gerry did boat chores while Dylan and I went fishing. Dad and Gerry were a good team. Gerry's hands were small but agile, and Dad was patient with him. Dad got done the things he wanted to do, and Gerry was learning—how to tie off a line, tighten a screw, handle the pliers—all the things Dad still had trouble doing. Dylan and I made a good fishing team. Dylan didn't want to use the gun, but he was good at spotting the best places to fish. I didn't have his eye for fish hideouts, but I had good aim and timing underwater. If we were lucky, we had fish for dinner. If not, we opened a can.

At Pigeon Cay, we were not lucky. Dylan and I took the dinghy out as usual, but soon clouds started piling up in the west, so we turned around and motored back to *Chrysalis*. When we got back, Dad and Gerry were not tinkering on the boat. They were reading in the cockpit, Gerry snuggled up next to Dad and leaning on his arm. Gerry was just finishing *Mike Mulligan* as the dinghy bow touched the stern.

I snagged the towline on the cleat. "I didn't know you could read."

"I'm learning," Gerry said. "In boat school."

I nodded, then checked the motor and tilted it forward. At home, everybody was settled into classes. The leaves were turning and the nights were getting sharp with cold. But we weren't at home. We were here. Instead of sitting in geometry class, we were plotting courses on a chart. Instead of memorizing biology vocabulary, we were learning about coral, conch, and fish. It was a strange sort of school, but there were parts of it I liked.

Dylan secured the oars and gas can under the seat.

"Get anything?" Dad said.

"No. Clouds," I answered, and pointed west.

"Too bad," Dad said, turning back to the books. "Okay. My turn again." He pulled his poetry book from under Gerry's stack of little-kid books and started reading in his poetry voice, kind of dreamy and heavy. "'Pain—has an Element of Blank—'" he read. "'It cannot recollect when it begun—or if there were a time when it was not—'"

I handed the speargun to Dylan.

"'It has no Future—but itself—'" his voice read. "'Its Infinite contain its Past—enlightened to perceive New Periods—of Pain.'"

When Dad was quiet, I looked up. He was reading the poem again silently to himself. "That was a real cheerful poem," I said.

"But true," Dad answered.

Gerry sat quietly, holding Blankie's silky corner against his leg and slowly rubbing it up and down.

"I didn't like that one," Gerry said. "Let's read this." He handed Dad *Where the Wild Things Are*.

As Dylan and I climbed into the cockpit, Dad looked up at me. "I must have read this book to you a thousand times, Ben."

Dylan sat down beside Gerry, and Dad's real voice began

to read about Max making mischief in his wolf suit.

I lay down on the cockpit cushions and closed my eyes.

Dad turned a page. "Look at that monster," he said.

I heard Dad's hand smoothing down the page and the shift as he and Gerry adjusted positions.

Pigeon Cay was not the best anchorage. The boat rocked a bit in the freshening breeze and the halyards clanged against the mast when the wake from a Bahamian fishing boat caught us. But now all that felt normal. When you live on a boat, your muscles are constantly adjusting to the moving ocean, but you never think about it. Not the moving or the noise—the pings and taps along the hull when you're lying in your bunk, the knocks and slaps and gurgles when you're in the cabin. You get used to it. I moved on the seat and felt the slight grit of sand and the stickiness of salt. Even that was normal now. I hardly noticed any of it anymore.

Dad's voice went on. The pages rustled as he and Gerry looked quietly at the pictures. I remembered stories. After dinner, Dad gave me a soldier bath—a wet washcloth and a crazy story about hardship in the desert. He dressed me in my Batman pajamas and we climbed onto my bed. I leaned against the muscle of his arm, which smelled a little like sweat and Dylan's baby powder. When Dad read stories from a book, he pointed at the pictures. When he made up his own stories, he didn't finish them.

"Once upon a time, a boy named Ben had a boat and he sailed away."

"Where to?"

"I don't know. That's your part of the story."

Sitting in the shade of the bimini on *Chrysalis*, he paused at the end of a page.

"The monsters are mean," Gerry said.

"You think so?" Dad asked.

Then Max said good-bye to the wild things, and they threatened to eat him up.

"We love you," they said, and I laughed again.

Max stepped onto his private boat and we all came sailing home with him, through a year and "in and out of weeks," and when I opened my eyes, it was still hot. Hot and about to rain. Gerry hopped down below with the books. Dylan and I piled the cockpit cushions under the bimini. The rain lasted only ten minutes, then Dad had us doing the end-of-storm routine. We opened all the hatches, dried the cockpit seats, set out the cushions, and hung the drying towel on the line. The rigging kept raining on us for a while. Big, fat, heavy drops fell—*plop*—right in the middle of the top of my head.

"Ben."

I turned and saw Gerry standing just behind me, Blankie draped around his neck and his hands hidden behind his back. He handed me a wadded-up piece of drawing paper.

"What's this?"

"Open it."

The paper was a little damp and tore as I pulled it open. Inside was one of Gerry's cars.

"Happy birthday," Gerry said.

"Surprise," Dylan said.

"Oh," Dad said. "I forgot."

"I did too," I said. I was sixteen now. "Thank you, Gerry," I said. I looked at the rusty little car sitting in the torn paper and closed my fist around the toy.

CHAPTER SEVENTEEN

WE LEFT ANDROS for Nassau in December. We came into the harbor from the west, threading our way through a cacophony of marine traffic—freighters, fishing boats, a sand dredge, private yachts, buzzing Jet Skis. We passed Prince George Wharf, which was wall-to-wall cruise ships, then sailed under the bridges and tied up at a marina just beyond Potters Cay. It was the first time *Chrysalis* had been in a slip since we left Marathon, and none of us liked it very much.

We hadn't finished tying off the lines when two little kids came running up with tiny straw baskets in their hands asking us to buy. When we said no and turned away, they just kept asking. We had to go down below before they would leave. Dad was writing a grocery list. He pulled some money from his wallet and handed it to me. "Take this list and find a grocery. All three of you. Go."

We hated Nassau. The crowds were too thick. The straw market was too fake. The cruise ships were too big. The casinos were too pink. Their palm trees were too perfect. The workers' smiles were too big. Everyone wanted to braid our hair or get us a cab—for a fee, of course. One guy tried to hustle me some marijuana. Gerry wouldn't let go of my hand. Dylan said it was time to find the grocery.

The sun glared off the buildings as we walked back in the noontime heat carrying the heavy bags. The breeze from the harbor was blocked until we walked by the fish market where we caught the sudden, powerful smell of dead fish. Fishermen stood in the sterns of their boats and hawked the piles of fish lying at their feet while the women sorted or bagged or cleaned them.

One guy had conch rolling around in the bottom of his boat. He picked up a conch and used the claw end of a hammer to whack a hole in the whorls at the top. He flashed a knife inside the hole and then grabbed the conch's crawling claw, yanking the animal out of its shell in one slimy gray blob. The whole process took about five seconds. He handed the flat, palm-size, alien-looking creature to the waiting customer, picked up another shell, and did it all over again in another five seconds flat. They exchanged money, the fisherman sucked on a beer, and another customer came up.

"That is the grossest thing I ever saw," I said.

"I'd like to try it," Dylan said.

"Is it dead when he pulls it out?" Gerry asked. "Or do you kill it afterward?"

"You guys are weird," I said, and we moved on.

When we got back, we noticed the oil slick on the marina water. Our own boat felt sticky and dirty. We were ready to leave and we hadn't been there six hours.

But like everything else, we started to get used to Nassau too. Dad was busy with boat repairs. He didn't like a noise the rudder was making, and he was worried our water tanks might be leaking. The radio was doing something funny again, and he had decided to replace the mainsail. The marina needed hands to scrape and paint boat bottoms, so Dad and I helped out. It paid our slip fee and grocery bills. Dylan and Gerry spent more time on schoolwork and wrote long letters to Aunt Sue and their friends at home. Dad said I should write too, maybe even to Andrew, but when I sat down with the paper, I couldn't think of anything to say. Everything would have been like speaking a foreign language.

In our downtime, Dad shopped for spare parts and canned goods, and we wandered the streets on our own. Right around the harbor, people weren't very friendly, but on the back streets, it was better. Ladies were always rubbing Gerry's hair because it was so white, but nobody noticed Dylan or me. We blended in pretty well. Our skin was as tanned as it could get and our hair was long. I had started wearing a bandanna to keep mine out of my face. Gerry said I looked like a pirate. Dylan said I looked like a rock star. Mainly we looked like boat bums, so nobody in Nassau noticed us.

Christmas came and Nassau had its own celebration the day after. They called it Junkanoo. We wanted to go, but Dad said no, the crowds would be too much. Then he changed his mind for the second Junkanoo parade on New Year's Day. When we arrived in the early morning, it was going strong. Costumes and dancing and music. Drums. Cowbells. Blowing on conch shells. A man did handstands down the street. A little boy sold conch fritters. Dad kept yelling at us to stay together.

I was beating my hand against my leg to the goombay rhythm and watching the girls running down the street, screaming and laughing and slapping each other, when a woman in a bikini top and a long skirt came dancing over to Dad and rubbed up against him. Dad gently pushed her away. She laughed and came dancing back. "Smile, man," she said. "It's a party." Dad turned away and she laughed again. "Are you afraid of me?" she asked. She put her arms around his waist and danced against him. "It's okay, man," she said. "Your wife's not here." Dad went rigid, then twisted out of her arms, and scooped up Gerry. He grabbed Dylan's arm and shouted at me to follow. We pushed our way back through the crowds and noise to the marina.

The quiet felt hollow. Dad eased himself down on the cockpit seat. Gerry stretched out beside him and picked at the threads coming out of the cushion covers. Dylan and I stood holding on to the backstay and watching Dad. He rubbed his hands up and down on his thighs. "That woman," he finally said. "I don't like crowds. I think it's time for us to go."

"Did you get the new sail yet?" Dylan asked.

"We don't really need it. It's too expensive anyway."

"The radio's fixed?" I asked.

"The guy came yesterday," he said.

We nodded. We all agreed.

So in the late morning of the first day of the new year, Dylan, Gerry, and I watched from the foredeck as the city slipped away. Gerry sat with Blankie clutched at his stomach. I coiled the dock lines. Dylan dropped the fenders into the forward hatch.

"Where are we going?" Gerry rubbed Blankie's silky corner against his cheek.

"North," I said. "To the Berry Islands."

He carefully wound Blankie around his hands. "Ben," he asked quietly, "how long has it been?"

I paused and looked at him. "Since what, buddy?"

He looked up at me, his face tightening against tears, and slid Blankie over his head.

Dylan and I looked at each other, then back at him.

"I want to go home," Gerry said, his voice quiet under Blankie.

"We're halfway there, buddy," I said. "We're halfway home."

CHAPTER EIGHTEEN

HUNDREDS OF ISLANDS make up the Bahamas, and in six months we had seen only a handful. In Nassau, Dad had laid the chart out on the table. To the east were Eleuthera and Cat Island. To the south, Long Island and the Exumas. Even farther south were the last scattered specks of Bahamian territory: Crooked and Acklins islands, Mayaguana, and Great and Little Inagua. Still farther south was the little nation of Turks and Caicos. Among these last scraps of land were islands where only a few people lived, as well as those occasional cays with no people at all and no names, either. There was no natural freshwater and no way to grow food. A boater couldn't stop and provision or fill up with water or fuel because there wasn't any. We had six months left. Dad didn't want to waste time in that desert area. He decided to skip the southern Bahamas.

Instead, we sailed north to the Berrys. There's not much there. Just one island after another strung out in a slow curve for twenty-five miles from Chub Cay in the south to Great Stirrup Cay in the north. Almost nobody lives there. Just birds and lizards and conch and lobster. The Berrys are lonely and beautiful.

It was there that we had the golden day. In my memory, this day is the brightest. A day with sunshine sparkling around our eyes. With glitter in the sand and with water dancing blue and clear all around the edges. The perfect day.

The day before, we had taken our longest sail since crossing the Bank. The last two hours were in rolling seas. We wedged ourselves in the cockpit to keep in one place, but Gerry was too short. Finally I just held him in my lap. We stared over the rails and waited for it to be over.

At last we were abreast of the turn and could clearly see the rock we were supposed to beware of. Dylan was shouting degrees through the companionway and Dad was barking back, "Double-check that course, Dylan. That can't be right." Then Dad turned on the engine to be sure it was ready when we got set to anchor, but it didn't start. So he started yelling at me and I started yelling at him. Dylan was quiet and Gerry was rolling around in the cockpit. It was really fun.

Then we turned *Chrysalis*'s bow into Little Harbour.

In an instant, the rolling stopped. All those waves were blocked now by a long, low island beside us. And in the middle was a calm green pool of ocean, the edges licking gently against a circle of little islands surrounding us.

We were quiet. We glided in under jib alone. Dad didn't yell. I scrambled to the bow and laid out the anchor chain. Dylan stood on alert beside the jib halyard. Quietly Dad said, "Dylan," and Dylan released the halyard. The jib tumbled in billows onto the deck. He gathered it neatly inside the lifelines. We were quiet again for a minute.

"Ben," Dad said, and I let the anchor go. The chain rattled out of the anchor locker and I counted the markers going by—ten feet, twenty feet, thirty feet—

Dad said nothing.

I saw the anchor sink into the sandy bottom. I snagged it tight. *Chrysalis* swung gently on her chain and slowly turned her bow into the wind. The quiet rolled over us like liquid. We sat there just looking out at the little circle of islands and feeling the gentle leftovers of breeze. It was peaceful; it was perfect; it was ours alone.

The next day we slept late—even Dad—and woke up only when we heard a voice calling, "Hello! Hello! Ahoy *Chrysalis.*" I heard Dad knocking against the hull as he woke up. He was at the companionway before I had pushed off my covers. By the time I sat up, he and Dylan were already on deck. I heard voices.

"De worse dat could happen," a Bahamian man said, and I was on deck too.

He stood in his dinghy, rowed by a single paddle astern, and held on to *Chrysalis*'s gunwale. Beside us now, in our perfect anchorage, was a Bahamian fishing boat. On the deck several fishermen lounged and watched their mate.

"De worse dat could happen, mon," he said again. "We have forgotten to bring de sugar for de tea."

And Dad laughed. He threw back his head and laughed. "Sugar!" he said. "I thought someone was dying. Ben, go get these guys some sugar. Lots of sugar."

Dylan and I looked at each other. He had said "dying." He had laughed.

I came back up with an unopened three-pound bag of sugar. Behind me came Gerry, wiping his eyes with Blankie.

"Tanks, mon," said the Bahamian. He looked at us. "Dese all yours, mon?"

"Every one," Dad said.

"You lucky," the fisherman said. "We catch some lobster, we'll bring you some."

"Sure," Dad said. "Sure."

The fisherman rowed away, standing in his boat, pushing the stern paddle from right to left and cradling the sugar in the crook of his arm.

Dad turned to us smiling. "Coffee?" he said, and the perfect day began.

What was so perfect about it? Just that it was. Dylan and I spent the morning in the dinghy, puttering around the end of one of our sheltering islands. Dylan was watching the bottom, looking for conch. After lunch, we took Gerry with us, and he leaned over to look too.

We rounded the end of one of the islands in the circle. Out there was the great wide sea, green and glittering and calm. To our right was a sudden crescent of sand no more than ten feet long. We beached the dinghy and sat there, the three of us, alone, looking out to sea.

In that moment, I imagined we were the only ones on earth. From where we sat on our miniature temporary beach, it was an easy thing to imagine. Except for the dinghy and the tiny whiff of exhaust and gas, there was no sign of human life. Before us lay the ocean, behind and around us the little scrub island. No Dad. No *Chrysalis*. No nothing. Just us and the waves and the fiddler crabs and the conch. I lay down and looked at the sky, and something in me felt light enough to rise right on up with the clouds and go spinning off in some kind of crazy, wild dance.

I jumped up. "Let's swim. Come on, Gerry. We'll teach you."

"Just a little, Ben," he said cautiously.

I felt so soft inside. "Okay, buddy. Bare butts, everyone."

So we stripped, laughing and poking. My brothers' skinny white butts looked like little rabbit behinds as they hopped into the water.

Gerry reached out for Dylan's hand and Dylan took it. They didn't look at each other. It was just electricity, I guess. I remembered Mom doing that. She could be looking 180 degrees away, and Gerry's hand would go out and hers would be right there—like she had some kind of radar or something. When I saw her in my mind like that, it wasn't sadness I felt. It was joy. This sudden bolt of joy.

So I ran into the water and tackled Dylan and splashed Gerry. I yelled and they started screaming and splashing. Gerry's head got wet before he thought about it and he was pushing himself on the bottom with his hands and kicking his feet.

"You're swimming," we yelled like wild hyenas, and launched ourselves backwards into the water. I picked up Dylan like a baby and pitched him thrashing and howling back into the water. He came up laughing and wanting more.

Gerry carefully tried coming deeper.

"You want me to throw you?" I asked.

"No."

So I didn't—just like that. Because he said no. "Okay, I'll hold you up to practice swimming." But I could see he didn't trust me.

So Dylan held him. I watched and played cheerleader. "Do your arms like this. Now kick. Try floating on your back. It's just like sleeping. Hold your arms out. Stick up your chin."

Before too long, Gerry was ready for Dylan to let go.

But he sank. I snatched him up and he came up with his eyes big and round and scared, wiping water off his face with his palms. Blowing and puffing, but not crying.

"I think he beat Mom's record for the fastest sinking ever," Dylan said, and we laughed.

"Want to try again?" I asked.

He shook his head.

And I almost remembered something. Like when you catch a whiff of something and your brain starts clicking like a motor trying to start. But it can't. You click and click and then it's lost. This time it felt like a cool breeze in the summer heat or a touch of shade in the summer sun. Something in it felt like closing my eyes and just drifting in cool calm. But I lost it, and as it floated away, I thought something in it was about Mom.

I waded back out of the water and sat on the beach, propping my arms on my knees, watching Dylan and Gerry play until I found myself staring at the sand between my knees and felt Dylan's fingers on my head.

They sat on either side of me. The quiet grew. A seagull squawked. The tiny waves kissed the beach. The lizards slithered behind us.

"Come on," Dylan said. "Tide's coming in."

I looked up and saw that the ocean was crowding out our little beach. The sand crescent was almost gone. Quietly we launched the dinghy. Quietly we puttered to the boat. Quietly we watched the sun set.

When night came, we sat in the cockpit with Dad and ate the lobster the fishermen had brought while we were playing in the water. Everyone had his own lobster tail. It was way too much. We were dripping butter down our chins and Dad was laughing at us. He kept telling Gerry to wipe his face and then wiping it for him.

It was fun. Sitting in the dark, dripping butter, and listening to Dad and Gerry laugh.

Dad asked us about our exploring mission, and Dylan told him about seeing the conch and finding the beach and going swimming.

"Ben made us take off our clothes!" Gerry said suddenly.

"You swam naked!" Dad said, pretending to be shocked.

Gerry nodded. "It was weird."

"But you like to swim naked," Dad said.

"I remember," Dylan said. "The beach at the lake."

Dad nodded. "Remember that green swimsuit with motorboats all over it?"

Boy! Did I remember! Gerry wouldn't wear anything else when he was two and it was way too big.

Dad was wiping the butter off his fingers. Then he turned and took Gerry's hands and started gently wiping the fingers one by one.

"Once upon a time," Dad said, "there was a boy named Gerry who always wore a green motorboat suit when he played in the water. Now Gerry had a teeny, tiny, baby bottom, and every time he stood up in the water the suit slipped right over his behind and down to his knees. An old man, who was Gerry's dad, fussed at a beautiful woman, who was Gerry's mom."

Did Dad really stop to catch his breath or did I imagine it?

"'The boy needs his string tied!' the old man said. Poor Gerry came to him, crying and dragging his suit around his ankles. The old man hoisted the suit, adjusted it around that teeny waist, and pulled on the strings. Nothing happened. The strings were just decoration!

"'Just go without,' growled the old man. But little Gerry refused. He cried and tried to play in the water while desperately holding up his suit. The beautiful lady laughed. The old man laughed. And little Gerry cried and cried."

Then Dad really did stop talking. He turned and looked straight at me.

"And suddenly," Dad said, "out of nowhere came Gerry's biggest brother. Within a second, the brother's suit was off and he had tossed it in a ball to the beautiful lady. He scooped up little Gerry. The middle brother caught Gerry's suit as it fell to the water and then stripped off his own suit and brought them both to his mom.

"And the three boys marched into the water butt naked. And the mom and dad weren't laughing. They were smiling and being very careful not to look at each other because their eyes were all glittery. Then the lovely lady's fingers touched the old man's hand and without turning her head, she said very quietly, 'I'm sure glad there's no one else at the beach today!'

"And then they laughed and laughed and the boys played and played. And that's the story of how Gerry learned to swim naked. The end."

"Is that true?" Gerry asked.

"Every word," Dad said, and leaned back to gaze at the sky. "Orion," he said. "Dylan, look. There's Orion."

Dylan looked. We all looked. Orion was bright, especially his belt.

I closed my eyes.

And that was the golden day. Afterward I remembered Orion and the dripping butter. I remembered the naked butts skipping into the water. I remembered the splashing, backwards free falls. I remembered that I had almost remembered, and I wondered what it was I had lost.

CHAPTER NINETEEN

BUT THE GOLDEN day ended. We bounced through the Berrys. Then we went farther north to the Abacos, the top of the Bahamas. We headed north along the cays on the eastern side of Great Abaco—Little Harbour, Man-O-War Cay, Green Turtle Cay.

Dad's hand was still bothering him. The scar site was tender, and the injured muscles refused to tighten enough to allow him to take a strong grip on a line. Fortunately, I was getting stronger. I didn't need his help anymore to get the main up the last few inches, and sometimes it was easier to tighten the genoa just by pulling on the line without using a winch handle. Dylan had gotten strong enough to manage the anchor, and Gerry had turned out to be good with a fishing pole. We got better and better at our new jobs as we cruised through the last few islands before we headed home.

At one island, we gathered lobster just like the Bahamians did. At another, we watched sharks cruising after a fishing boat. At another, we found a coconut and ate it. At one island, Gerry turned six and we remembered to say happy birthday. Each island was small and perfect. Each one was our anchorage for days and days.

Then we stopped at Spanish Cay. It was beautiful just like all the others. Lonely, small, and empty. Dad and I could do the double-anchor trick now without using the dinghy if the harbor was big enough or empty enough. We sat in the cockpit eating lunch and dozing in the midday sun. Dad finished his drink, crumpled his napkin, and tossed it in the trash. "Boys," he said. "I've made up my mind."

I was lying on the port side of the cockpit. I opened my eyes and looked at him. Dylan turned from where he was sitting on the stern, hanging his legs over the side. Gerry pulled his legs up under him and twisted Blankie around his hands.

"About what?" I finally asked when Dad didn't speak again.

"You are an excellent crew," he said. "Ben, you're a born sailor. Dylan, your navigation is perfect. Gerry, you try hard and you're learning. I've watched you all and I know you can handle it. You're the best."

I sat up. Dylan moved to the cockpit.

"And *Chrysalis* is a good boat. She's not pretty and she's not new, but she's strong and seaworthy. She can take us anywhere."

"What are you saying?" I asked.

"I'm saying," Dad said, "that if we wanted to, we could cross the Atlantic Ocean. We could sail around the world."

Hot sun filled up the cockpit. I felt the sweat under my arms. "But we don't want to," I said.

"No," Dad said. "Not now. But later. First, we'll just go to Bermuda. Tomorrow we'll turn back to Marsh Harbour. We need to get the radio repaired. That guy in Nassau didn't know what he was doing. And I'm still not happy about that noise in the rudder. So we'll spend a few days in Marsh Harbour making repairs and stocking up. Then we'll head to Bermuda. It's not quite nine hundred miles from here. It'll take us five to seven days to get there, I'd guess."

"You're joking," I said.

"No," Dad said. "I'm perfectly serious. Look what we've done, what we've learned. Now we have a chance to do even more, learn even more."

"What about money?"

"We'll work. People do that. Like we did in Nassau. You work where you go, and if you don't like it, you leave. I could probably teach in Bermuda. You guys could sit in a classroom if you wanted, or we could keep on with the homeschooling. It wouldn't matter. After storm season ended, we could go to—I don't know—Spain maybe. Learn Spanish. Or to Portugal, where the great sailors came from." He laughed. "It's what I've always wanted to do, and now we can do it." He stood up. "Storm's coming, boys. Better get the boat ready."

He went down below, but we couldn't move.

Gerry held Blankie pressed against his mouth. Dylan twisted in his seat and looked out at the water.

A small sailboat quietly motored into the harbor. We watched the couple drop their anchor, bring up drinks, and sit to rest under their bimini.

The wind picked up suddenly. *Chrysalis* started rolling. The couple scrambled down below, but we were still frozen.

Dad poked his head out of the companionway.

"You said one year," I said.

"Get moving," he said. "We don't want everything to get wet."

We swung into action, doing storm routine in double time. We saw the line of the rain passing through the entrance to the harbor and had our boat locked up tight and storm-safe before the first drops hit. Down below, nobody spoke. Gerry got out his clothespins and acorns and started a war in his bunk. Dylan was flipping the pages in his star book. Dad was reading, but I guessed it wasn't poetry this time.

I sat at the navigation table and looked at the chart. Spanish Cay was part of a curve of islands arching across the northern rim of the Bahamas. We had been sailing west, closer every day to Walker's Cay, the northwesternmost island in the Bahamas. I had thought we would spend some time there, maybe even a long time, and then sail the final leg, less than two hundred miles back across the Gulf Stream to Florida—and then home.

It was the obvious thing to do. He had said a year, and by

the time we made it back to Florida, it would be almost a year. We had learned the things we needed to learn. We had had the adventures. Sometimes we had even had fun.

"Dad," I said, and turned to look into his bunk.

He was lying on his side gazing out his porthole. The rain thrummed on the deck above us.

"You can't do this," I said. "You can't just decide."

He opened his mouth to speak, but I went on. "It's just like before. You can't just—"

Then the other boat hit us. Dad thunked against the side of the boat and Gerry fell out of his bunk. A wave lifted us apart, and then the other boat got us again. I fell out of my seat and hit the cabin sole on my knees. We heard screaming voices, and Dad and I were out in the cockpit before either of us said anything more. The little boat, about two-thirds our size, was dragging her anchor and broadsiding our stern. Dad and I were hauling out the fenders and Dad was cursing the other sailors.

"Get your motor on!" he screamed.

The guy in the other boat was fumbling with his engine and shouting instructions to the woman. She was looking for their fenders and dropping lines all over the cockpit floor. The rain was sheeting down.

The seas lifted them toward us again. They came from slightly above and then raked down across our stern, their lifelines momentarily catching on our stern rail. The pressure of their boat against ours ripped the fender out of my hands before I could tie it off on the lines. Dad grabbed the boat hook and held it out like a spear to push the other boat away.

The boat rose and came at us again. The thud caught Dad off balance and knocked him flat. He lost his grip on the boat hook and it went flying into the cockpit, whacking Dylan on the head just as he and Gerry stumbled through the companionway hatch.

"Stay below! You'll get hurt!" Dad yelled at them. "Just lie down on the cabin floor."

They scrambled back down as the other boat's engine finally chugged into life. Dad was yelling at them not to cut our anchor lines as they motored away from us, pulling up their own useless anchor and screaming at each other. They had no choice now but to motor out of the harbor. The rain was already much lighter, but the space was too small and the sea too rough for them to try anchoring again.

Dad threw himself down on the cockpit seat in the rain puddles. He leaned back on his elbows and let the thick drops fall straight into his face. I stood on the stern in the rain, holding on to the backstay and concentrating on the up-and-down motion of the ocean rolling under us. Dad and I were breathing hard and our clothes were wet to the skin. Then Dylan's and Gerry's faces appeared like twin moons in the dark square of the companionway hatch.

"Are we going to sink?" Gerry asked.

"No." Dad was short with him. "Of course not." He roused himself and leaned over the stern to look.

We all looked.

"It's just scratches, Dad," Dylan said.

The collision had taken out part of the name painted on the stern. Now it said *Chrys—is.*

Dad looked at that for a few minutes, then answered Dylan. "Yes. Just scratches, a fender, and the GPS antenna."

The sensor for our navigation system was usually hanging there attached to the stern rail. Now it was gone.

Gerry looked at the empty space. He sat down in the cockpit and slowly pulled Blankie over his head.

"Don't worry," I said. "We'll replace it in Marsh Harbour."

Dad snorted. "You've obviously never been to Marsh Harbour."

White heat rolled over me like a tidal wave as I turned to speak to Dad. "You're right," I said. "I haven't ever been to Marsh Harbour, and I never want to go to Marsh Harbour. Not now. Not ever."

"Then we won't," Dad said evenly.

I could feel the adrenaline pumping into the tips of my fingers. I could feel the rush in the soles of my feet.

"We're going home?" I asked.

"No," Dad said. "We'll head straight for Bermuda and replace the GPS antenna there. We'd have to order a new one in Marsh Harbour and have it mailed. It could take weeks. The season's closing in. We don't need to waste time in Marsh Harbour waiting for what we can buy in half an hour in Bermuda."

He bent to gather the remaining fenders.

"What about the radio?" Dylan asked. "That guy in Nassau didn't fix it. It still goes in and out."

"Why don't you look at it, Ben?" Dad started. "You're good with—"

"Sorry. I don't do radios. Just engines. You said the guy in Marsh Harbour could fix it."

"The guy in Bermuda can fix it. We can pick up the weather report fine. That's all that matters."

"Exactly how do you plan to find Bermuda without a GPS?"

"Dead reckoning," Dad said. "Dylan and I can both easily get us to Bermuda."

"You're crazy," I said. "I thought you were better, but you're not. You're still crazy. You want us to sail out into the middle of the ocean with a broken radio and a busted navigation system because you're angry at some stupid stranger. Well, we're not doing it. We're not leaving for Bermuda in the morning. We're going home."

Dad stood and tossed the fender to me. I caught it.

"Stow it," he said.

"No," I said, and dropped the fender on the deck.

Dad stood on the back of the boat and looked over our heads. He was so still, I could see that he was trembling all over. "I am the captain," Dad said. "We will sail for Bermuda in the morning."

"No!" I screamed. "Not this time. You can't make us go this time."

Then suddenly Dad raised his hand and slapped me hard across my face.

"Stop!" Dylan shouted. "Please stop."

"Don't stop!" I yelled, my face stinging as Dad raised his hand again. "Go ahead. Hit the other side."

Then from under Blankie came Gerry's little voice. "I can see you," he said. "Did you know that?"

Dad jerked back his hand and looked at Gerry sitting there like a Halloween ghost.

"Blankie is so thin, I can see right through him."

Dad's face pinched. He turned his back on us and leaned over the stern, holding on to the lifelines. Then he threw up. Just like that. *Whomp*. Right into the ocean.

"You're sick," Dylan said.

"No," Dad said. He straightened up, looking a little white. "I am not sick." Then he looked at me. "And I am not crazy."

I felt prickles like fear in the hair on the back of my neck.

"I am a very lonely man—who wants his wife back."

"Dad—" I started.

"Just shut up," he shot back. "For once can you just shut up."

Dylan handed him a cloth to wipe his face.

Dad rubbed his mouth and chin, then threw the cloth in the water. "We'll sail tomorrow," he said. "We'll be fine."

So the next day we set sail for Bermuda. If we had had more time, if the storm hadn't come just then, if the other boat hadn't hit us, if I hadn't gotten so angry—maybe we could have talked. Maybe we could have changed his mind.

But it all happened so fast. One minute I was thinking we were heading home. Then the next minute I was lashing the dinghy over the forward hatch and hauling up the sails as we turned *Chrysalis* toward Bermuda, farther from home than ever.

We sailed on Dylan's sun shots all that first day. At night Dad set watches. The second day was easy too. Bright and sunny. I went to bed that second night with Dylan at the helm holding a compass course of thirty-five degrees north-northeast. We were making about six knots. Bermuda was only a few more days away. I figured that after we'd been there a while, we could talk to Dad and he would change his mind. In the meantime, he was right—the compass was as good as the electronics. We were going to make it. We were going to make it easily.

But we didn't. We never reached Bermuda. And it wasn't because we got lost. It was because we lost Dad.

THE STORM

CHAPTER TWENTY

ON THE THIRD morning at sea I woke up and heard the boat. When you've been on a boat for a while, its sound gets to be like the sound of your own heartbeat. It's always there, constant and steady, until after a while you don't hear it anymore. Then something changes. The speed, or the rhythm, or the tune. Suddenly the sound rings in your ears.

That morning when I woke up the boat sounded different. It felt different. The sails were slapping in and out, and we were wallowing between the waves. The wind had died or Dad had headed up into the wind on purpose. Maybe something had snapped and he needed the pressure off the sails to fix it. That was easy to imagine after the whacks we took a few days before in Spanish Cay.

I rolled over in my berth. Eight o'clock. I had missed my

whole watch. Dad hadn't waked me. I put the pillow over my head.

"Thanks," I said to the pillowcase.

The sails slapped. We rode sideways between the waves. I heard a winch handle scrape across the cockpit floor next to my head. Whatever was broken was taking a while to fix. I listened for Dad's footsteps on the bow. The boat was quiet. The winch handle skidded again.

I sat up. I figured Dad was waiting for me to come up. When I appeared, he'd be bleary-eyed, repairing a sail maybe, feeling so self-reliant and self-sufficient, the sailor's palm fitted over his hand, the huge needle going up and down. If I wasn't impressed, I thought, he'd probably get angry.

I threw the pillow off and dragged on some shorts. I rubbed my face hard with my palms. "Okay," I said. "I'm impressed. I am really impressed."

I swung myself through the companionway and blinked in the sun. At home, eight o'clock seemed early. The sun just barely reached in between the buildings and under the trees. But here, nothing blocked the eight o'clock sun. It was already hot and bright. Here even the eight o'clock sun could burn you.

"Morning," I said as I stepped into the cockpit.

The cockpit was empty, but the autopilot was still connected, still whining and grinding, still trying to steer the old course in this different wind.

I turned toward the bow with my "Golly, I'm impressed" face fixed on tight.

Before the jib slapped across the bow, I thought I caught a glimpse of Dad bending under the bow pulpit, as if he were looking for something in the water. Then the sail popped back and I realized it was an illusion.

"Dad," I called, looking around the deck.

There was no answer except the autopilot. I hadn't realized how much noise it made when it was trying to steer an impossible course.

The deck was clearly empty.

I felt a little chill. Suddenly I thought maybe I had really seen him and he'd fallen overboard at just that second. I thumped to the bow. No Dad. There had been no splash anyway. As quiet as everything was, I would have heard him calling. And we weren't moving in the water. He would be right there beside the boat.

So where was Dad? Why was the autopilot on? And why hadn't he waked me?

I turned to go back to the cockpit and noticed the dinghy. The bow line and one stern line were untied. Why would Dad do that? If he was hiding under there, something was really wrong.

I knelt quickly and slowly lifted up the dinghy. Nothing was there, not even the emergency pack. What had Dad done with that? When we were under way it was never supposed to be moved. I scanned the deck. No pack anywhere.

Why was the dinghy loose? What had happened to the pack? And where was Dad?

I went below and checked his bunk. No Dad. I could have bounced a quarter on the sheets. His poetry collection was lying smack in the middle of his pillow.

Nowhere to hide in the main cabin, either.

Not in the V-berths. Dylan was snoring away up there alone.

Not squirreled away in the engine room. Not scrunched into the hanging locker. I eased past Dylan and gently opened the sail locker. The big orange bags were stowed in exactly the order Dad had commanded. Nothing there but sails.

The boat wallowed. The sails banged. The autopilot whined. I realized my blood was rushing in my ears. It was so loud I almost didn't hear Dylan's whisper.

"What's wrong, Ben?"

I jumped and banged my head.

"Nothing!" I rubbed my head while Dylan waited and I cursed.

Then I looked at him. "You want to know what's wrong?" I said. "Well, I'll tell you. Dad has disappeared. Gone! Vamoose!"

"What are you talking about?"

I felt suddenly dizzy and sat on his bed. "I'm talking about the fact that Dad is nowhere on this boat. He's gone."

Dylan sat up. He pulled on his shorts and rubbed his face.

"Don't wake up Gerry," he said. "He'll be scared. Let's go look again."

"Gerry will be scared. And you're not?"

"Shhh," Dylan said.

He tiptoed past Gerry's bunk and up onto the deck.

Eight o'clock is hot. Eight thirty is hotter. The wind had almost completely died, and the air was heavy. The rollers were smooth and glassy across their curving backs.

"Dad!" Dylan called. I guess he figured I hadn't thought of doing that.

"His cup," Dylan said. And it was. His coffee cup, half-empty and cold.

"His lifeline," he said, and was right again. Dylan held up the end attached to the boat. The other end was supposed to be hooked to Dad's safety harness, but he had taken it off. In the middle of a night watch. Alone. Why?

The autopilot ground and whined in the wallows.

"Look at the dinghy," I said.

He went forward and lifted it just as I had. "Where's the pack?"

"Don't know."

We sat in the cockpit. I picked up the winch handle before it slid across the floor again. The sails cracked against themselves. I turned off the autopilot and disconnected it. The air filled up with silence. The tiller bounced against my thigh. I grabbed it and held it still.

"What was our heading supposed to be?" I asked Dylan.

"Thirty-five degrees north-northeast."

"We have to make a one-eighty," I said. I made sure the

engine was in neutral and started it. The engine sputtered, then settled into its rhythm. Now we were wallowing in diesel fumes too.

"Lower the jib?" Dylan asked.

"No. Let's see what it does on the new course."

He turned to handle the lines as we swung around. I reached for the mainsheet, pulling the sail in hard. The mechanical purr of the ratchet block tightening down sounded like normal life, like an afternoon sail on the lake. I snagged *Chrysalis*'s mainsheet in the cleat and shifted the engine to forward. With a little way on, I slowly eased her around to 215 degrees.

We adjusted the sails to the whisper of wind and I killed the engine.

Dylan looked past me to the ocean. Our wake still showed in the smooth rolling sea. "I'll double-check the course," he said, and backed into the dark below.

I could hear Dylan searching the boat again. I heard him opening the lockers and the engine room and climbing around in Dad's bunk. Then he was quiet, and I was sitting there alone in the middle of a huge, round ocean under a brilliant dome of sky. There was nothing, nothing in sight except the monotonous curve of the waves and the occasional blinding glint of sunlight on the water.

We both knew it was impossible. Even if we could go back toward Spanish Cay at exactly the same angle as we had left it, we would be tracing a different line. We had no way of knowing how far east or west we were of our original path. And we didn't know how long Dad had been overboard. How long had he been drifting in the current? How long had we been wallowing without wind?

Then Dylan reappeared. He was holding a piece of paper and Dad's poetry collection. His lips were almost white.

"Ben," he said. He held up the paper, and I saw it was a letter in Dad's handwriting. "It's a letter to Mom."

CHAPTER TWENTY-ONE

DYLAN HANDED ME the letter. I didn't want to read it, but I did. It wasn't what I expected. It was a poem, but not from Dad's collection. He started out with her name, just "Christine." Then he wrote:

We danced in the dark and called it our song.
The sad, simple words you whispered low.
"Lonely" and "time" and "hunger" and "home"
Misunderstood then—now I know.

I am the river. You are the sea.
Open your arms, love—wait for me.

I read it through twice, then crushed the paper into a tight ball. "It's a suicide note," I said.

"It's about a song," Dylan answered. He took the paper from me and carefully began to pick open the ball.

"But listen to the words," I said. "He says she's the sea. He says she should open her arms."

"They had the CD." He flattened the paper against his thigh. "They listened to that song all the time."

"Rivers flow into the sea, Dylan. And he's gone into the sea. In the middle of the night. He unhooked his harness. He—"

Dylan bent slightly to look down at the note, held smooth against his thigh by his boy hands. When his hair fell forward slightly, I saw the smooth curve of his neck rising from his shoulder.

"Dylan," I started again.

He looked up. "Shush," he said, and tucked the letter back into the book.

Gerry had appeared in the companionway. He was holding Blankie bunched up under his chin. He didn't say anything. He stepped out, barefoot and wearing his Batman underwear. They were baggy in the seat—too big. Mom had planned a little too far ahead with them. Gerry sat by Dylan, then lay down on his side, curled around his stomach. He took a corner of Blankie and gently rubbed the silk against his cheek. He crossed his feet over each other. His breath came steady and even. His cheek was so smooth. His eyes staring across the deck were so quietly pale. I could have counted each rib, each vertebra. He couldn't float because he had no body fat.

Looking at Dylan and Gerry, I felt I could scream loud enough for Dad to hear me wherever he was. I felt I could climb to the top of the mast and yell at the sky. I felt I could terrify the depths of space with the scream inside me.

Gerry was watching me watch him. "What's wrong, Ben?" he asked.

I looked away. I picked up the book with the stupid letter sticking out the top. I slammed it onto the seat cushion.

"I hate him," I said.

"Don't say that," Dylan said.

Gerry sat up straight, alert, looking at the book in my hands. "Where's Dad?" he asked me.

I bit my lip.

"Dylan." Gerry's little voice was shaking. "Where's Dad?"

I stood up and headed down below. Dylan picked up a corner of Blankie and rubbed Gerry's other cheek. Gerry was already crying when I laid myself out on Dad's bunk with his pillow over my head and his book pressing a square hole in my chest.

CHAPTER TWENTY-TWO

I HAD GONE TO sleep again and was dreaming I was suffocating with that pillow over my head when Dylan shook my foot. "Wake up," he said. "We need to talk."

I rolled over and remembered everything all at once.

"Talk," I said, and followed Dylan into the cabin. Gerry was on deck holding the tiller with one hand and Blankie with the other. Beside him sat a can of orange juice. Dylan had spread the charts out on the chart table.

"We need to figure out where we are—or were—so we can figure out where we're going."

I rubbed my face hard with the palms of my hands. "We're lost," I said. "The GPS is broken, and we've been drifting in the sea in an unknown direction at an unknown speed for an unknown period of time."

There were simply too many variables. When Dad went overboard, the boat sailed on alone for a while, the autopilot maintaining a perfect course. Then, at some point, the wind changed and the boat stopped moving forward. It just rolled and wallowed wherever the wind and waves took it. But when did Dad go over? What speed was the boat going then? When did the wind change? What direction had it come from since then? How strong? Did it change again? There were too many things we didn't know.

"We're lost," I repeated, and sat down.

Dylan ignored me and sat at the chart table making dots with the pencil, drawing lines with the parallel rule, and calculating speed. Then he paused and glanced toward Gerry at the helm. "I told him we were going back to get Dad."

"In other words, you lied," I said.

Dylan's mouth tightened. "What would you have said?"

I kicked at a pencil that had dropped on the floor.

"Besides," Dylan went on, "Dad has the EPIRB. If we don't find him, someone else will."

I stared at Dylan. "What makes you think a man trying to drown himself would turn on the EPIRB?"

Dylan looked squarely back at me. "What makes you think he was trying to drown himself?"

"For crying out loud, Dylan! You read the note. Why would he do any of the things he's done? He's crazy and selfish and scared. And by now, he's probably dead. Just like he wanted to be."

"You're wrong," Dylan said quietly.

"Did you hear anyone call?" I asked. "Did you?"

"No."

"Don't you think he would have yelled if he had wanted help?"

"We were asleep."

"Grow up, Dylan," I said, and bent to pick up the pencil I had kicked.

When I sat up again, he was looking at the chart. "I made a note here last night," he said, "at the end of my watch." He carefully placed the pencil point on a dot well northeast of Spanish Cay. "We were going about four and a half knots on a heading of thirty-five degrees north-northeast. If the boat kept on for another two hours, it would have been about here"—another touch with the pencil—"when Dad went overboard." He paused. "But we have to figure in current. The water is moving over the ground at about five knots. We were moving through the water at four and a half knots."

Dylan's pencil worked some more. He swung the dividers along a line he'd drawn. "Okay, so we'd have been about here when he went over."

Dylan made a new dot and erased the other one.

"If he jumped at two o'clock," I said.

"Fell," Dylan answered.

I shrugged. "But what if it was twelve thirty? Or three o'clock? Or six o'clock?"

Dylan's boy fingers crunched around the pencil. "You want me to figure all those, too?"

"No."

"I can."

"I know you can. You're brilliant. But it doesn't matter. Dad is still gone, and we still don't know where we are."

"No." Dylan drew a thin squiggly line along the margin of the chart. "We're lost."

I flopped back against the settee. "We don't know where we are. So we can't know where we're going. Depending on where we started from, we could land right smack in the harbor at Spanish Cay in seventy-two hours. Or we could slide right between Florida and Cuba and end up on the Yucatan Peninsula. Or I suppose we could be farther east than that and miss the Bahamas altogether and end up in Turks and Caicos or the Dominican Republic. All of them are lovely destinations. I leave it to you to choose." I thumped the pencil against the cushion. "If he had just made a note of the time. If he had only kept up the log."

Dylan worked on his line.

"He should have thought about us," I continued quietly. "He should have—"

"If it had been on purpose," Dylan said, "he would have."

I looked up and saw Gerry standing at the helm. His hair was so blond it looked white in the sun. But the light around him seemed funny. I stood up to see the horizon. There wasn't one. The line where sea and sky should meet had disappeared in a broad black swath. The edge of the black clouds billowed out toward us. They stretched all the way across the ocean. From end to end. Rolling over the water and filling up the sky.

Dylan stood beside me. We looked at the storm coming.

Gerry was watching us, his sun-browned hand and overgrown fingernails scratching at his thigh.

Something stronger and colder than I'd ever felt was holding on to my insides. I felt the hair rise up on my neck and chills riding down my spine.

"Dylan," I asked, not daring to turn my eyes away, "do any of the books say what to do with this?"

"What is this?" he asked very quietly.

I held on to the companionway rail. "I think," I said, "that it's the end of the world."

CHAPTER TWENTY-THREE

DYLAN AND I stood frozen for long enough to die and come back to life. I lost the feeling in my fingertips. Then thick fat raindrops began to drop on the boat, and the wind freshened. We'd done storm drill at anchor a thousand times, but never at sea. I didn't know what to do.

"We'll just keep our course," I told Dylan, "and ride it out."

"What about Dad?" Dylan asked.

I didn't answer. I shrugged on my foul weather gear and handed Dylan his.

"I guess I know two things about storms," I finally said. "The first thing is you want to go just the right speed. You don't want to go so fast down into the trough of a wave that your bow plows into the ocean. It would be like putting on the brakes on your bike's front wheel. You'd pitchpole—flip upside down, front first. And you don't want to go so slow that a wave crashes on your stern and flips you over backwards."

Dylan nodded.

"The second thing," I said, "is that you want to stay pointed in the right direction. You don't want to get sideways to the waves. You have no stability that way. The waves will broadside you, and you'll broach—go over sideways."

Gerry was standing now, looking from us to the cloud behind him. The wind was beginning to whip his hair and twist his shirt against his chest. "Ben! Dylan! Look!"

"Hold on. We're coming, bud."

Behind Gerry the advancing wall of rain shattered the silvery surface of the water into a rolling layer of flat, pockmarked tin. I turned to Dylan. "I just thought of a third thing I know. You don't want to hit any land."

"Or coral heads," Dylan said, and we came out into the cockpit.

I leaned close to Gerry and shouted, "Hold your course, buddy. A few more minutes. We've got to get the jib down. Then I'll take over."

Dylan and I hooked our safety harnesses on the lifelines and started for the foredeck. The wall of rain struck. We fell to our knees and crawled. I popped the halyard off the cleat and kept the tension until Dylan was crouched at the foot of the sail. The forepeak rose off a wave, then slammed down. Dylan held on and looked back at me, his lips grim and tight. I released the halyard, but the jib only sagged. The wind held it up long enough for me to make my way to the forepeak too. Then the sail began to fall in great heavy folds, stiff and salty. Dylan took the clew and began pushing the sail into the sail bag. I wrestled with the hanks until the whole sail was unhooked and stuffed into the big orange bag. We shoved it through the forward hatch and turned to the dinghy, now twisting back and forth on the single line holding it on deck. We tied it down then crawled back to the cockpit.

I felt my hand closing around the tiller. I saw Gerry's eyes.

"What about Dad?" he yelled. "How can we find Dad?"

I didn't answer him. He was soaked. His hair looked dark stuck to his head. He grabbed my arm.

"What about Dad, Ben?"

"Go below," I yelled. "Get dry. Stay in your bunk."

He still held my arm. He was shivering.

He turned his face up at me again, and I saw he was crying. His mouth was a wide, dark square and his eyes were big.

I shook off his arm and pushed him. He stumbled and sat just in front of the companionway. "Go below!" I yelled.

"But what about Dad!" he wailed.

"Forget Dad!" My voice sounded high and shrill in the wind. Dylan's hand reached out and pulled Gerry inside, then slotted in the boards to close off the hatch.

I was alone on deck in the dark of the storm. The boat rode up the back of a wave and crashed down into the trough.

I yanked the mainsheet loose and held it while I steered. I worked the sheet and the tiller together until I had the boat in a carefully balanced reach heading southeast. We would make it. We were under control. It would be hard, but we would make it.

"Forget Dad," I said again. Then louder. As loud as I could. Out to the storm, the wind, the rain. Over and over again as I held us together, Dylan and Gerry and me, safe on the boat and screaming toward home.

CHAPTER TWENTY-FOUR

IT WAS GOOD sailing. The wind changed from northwest to north and I loosened up to a beam reach with the wind coming over our starboard rail. We climbed the backs of the waves at an angle then plowed down the fronts, cutting a deep wake across the sea. I sat high on the starboard side, wedging myself in so I couldn't slide. We were heeled over with water frothing over the port rail and spray flying back from the bow to wash over the deck and splash into my face.

It was like driving a car on a tight curve—fast. My focus narrowed to the feel of the vibrating tiller, the bounce of the white compass needle, and the tremble of the mainsail's leech. The tiller was like my body, attached to the rudder and sensing the pull of the boat, the nudging way she wanted to turn and head into the wind—just the way a car wants to pull a little to the right. You feel it without feeling it. It's part of the way you drive. It comes from your body, not your head. Either you can do it or you can't.

I could do it. And I could do it well. The wind tore past me, the waves rolled under me, the rain poured down on me, but I ignored them. There was only the pull, the bounce, and the tremble. I kept them in perfect balance. Sailing on the edge. Smiling.

But control is an illusion, and in a storm it is a dangerous illusion. You might forget to keep checking things. You might not notice the changes, and storms change. This one did, and I didn't notice. I was too busy thinking it was a good thing, that we'd get home sooner this way. Then the wind got stronger. I was fighting the boat harder. The rail never came out of the water. I was standing with my feet braced on the side of the port seat, clinging to the starboard lifeline with my right arm and fighting the tiller with my left. We sliced through the tops of the waves and surfed down the far side.

I felt an edge of fear start to blur my focus. "Think," I told myself. "You're going too fast. What do you do now? Think." But I was telling myself to think rather than doing it because there was nothing I could do. It was too late. We had too much sail up. It was like having the accelerator jammed to the floor and a mountain road in front of you. We should have reefed the main or taken it down. I should have thought of that.

Reefing the main was just a way of making the sail small-er. To reef the main in this old boat required first lifting the boom up so the bottom of the sail folded in a big loose flap. Then someone had to stand on the cabin roof and tie the bottom folds of the sail tightly to the boom. Meanwhile, of course, someone else was steering the boat. That would have been hard enough to do in this storm, but there was a worse problem. The first step in reefing was to center the boom over the cabin or at least pull it in close enough to reach it from the deck. That necessarily meant that the sail would also be centered over the boat—and taking the wind full into its belly. The boat would broach. Before we could even start tying the straps, the boat would be upside down in the ocean.

So we could not reef the main. Nor could we lower it. To loosen the pressure on the sail enough to allow it to slide down, we had to turn the boat into the wind. If we tried that, at some point the boat would be sideways to the wind and waves. Again, before I could get a good hold on the main, we'd broach. Knockdown. Three drowned sailors.

The speedometer was pegged at twelve knots. If we didn't slow down, we were going to plow straight into the wave in front of us and pitchpole forward. The huge white triangle of sail stood out against the dim light that was not night but black day. The wind howled after us, but there was no place to hide. No key to take out. No dream to wake up from. I had made a mistake and we were stuck with it. All of us—together.

CHAPTER TWENTY-FIVE

I LOST THE ABILITY to think. I wanted to call Dylan up to tell him, but I couldn't move and I couldn't yell loud enough to make him hear. What was the point anyway? I would just be telling him so I would have somebody else be as scared as I was.

And they were probably scared enough already, stuck down below in their bunks with no light. They couldn't see the storm, only hear it and feel the pounding on the boat and the sharp heel to port. I hoped they were wedged in somehow. Two hot bodies in the dark of a tiny boat smashed by the waves and wind. All they could do was wait. I wondered if Gerry was crying—or if he was too scared even for that.

And still *Chrysalis* tore through the waves, black in the half-light except where they foamed yellow over and past the hull.

The wind shrieked through the stays and shoved the waves up higher and higher until the tops blew off and fell raining into the cockpit. The waves grabbed for the forepeak, then picked up the bow and slammed it down in the troughs. *Chrysalis* shuddered with every blow, every joint in her hull loosening. We were taking in water somewhere, but I couldn't go look. I could only steer and look at the sail, stretched by the screaming wind to a big, round, peculiar shape.

Then something exploded. Suddenly. Like a bomb detonated right on our deck. A crack, a boom, a roar of sound that knocked me backward and drowned out the shriek of the wind as the echoes reverberated in my head.

The sail. Our sail had exploded, ripped to shreds by the wind's pressure. The leading edge hugging the mast was still intact, but the leech was torn into a string of ridiculous signal flags flashing mindlessly at the storm. The boom swung wildly while yards of canvas hung from it, dragging across the cockpit and dipping into the sea.

I stared. One second we were screaming along with the sail bellied out tight and whole. The next, the sail was gone and the boat was stalled, turning slowly sideways to the waves.

I didn't have to call Dylan. The hatch boards were flying out of the companionway, and he was climbing into the cockpit as I hauled in the boom and pulled the longest shreds out of the water. Dylan didn't need me to explain anything. He saw immediately what had happened. He turned and motioned Gerry back down. I pointed to the tiller and yelled, "Keep the wind behind us. Keep the waves coming from the stern."

I found the longest line we had in the cockpit locker and stood. Just as I looked at Dylan, a wave broke over the stern, dropping gallons of water straight down on us. I lost sight of Dylan for that instant. Then he was there again. Wet. Water running off his nose. And trembling slightly. I turned to go forward. My plan was simple. Lower the mainsail and tie the shreds to the boom. Under the conditions, it was an impossible plan.

I crawled along the edge of the boat. I could have brushed the rushing, bubbling water with my fingers if I could have let go to reach out.

When I got to the mast, I crawled slowly up to the center of the boat. I lodged the line between my knees and the mast and took hold of the main halyard to release it. My fingers were cold and felt like exposed bone. I picked at the wet, stiff line. It wouldn't give. Then suddenly it let go, and the force of the heavy slapping shreds of sail against the line almost jerked me up. I used the cleat as a pulley and let the sail down slowly.

As it lowered, it billowed out with the wind. Dylan tugged at the tiller to meet this new force. Then the sail was completely down, its acres of white canvas heaving in the wind, the torn edges flashing up and slapping at the deck.

I clung to the mast with both arms while the boat twisted back and forth, trying to throw me into the sea. I knew I had to let go with one arm. I had to gather the sail and tie it off. A pinpoint in my mind again thought of Gerry down below. Where could he be wedged? How frightened must he be?

I held on with my left arm and crushed down the sail with my right. I tied one end of the line around that first hump of broken sail. Then I stepped aft six inches and crushed, again and again, wrapping the line in a spiral around the flapping, soaked edges of the shredded sail as I hauled them in inch by inch and pound by pound and beat them into a sodden lump on top of the boom.

I couldn't feel my left arm anymore. It was just a hook that I slid along the boom to hold me on. The muscles in my right arm were past exhausted and moved like a machine. I caught every flap, every shred. I was screaming at the sail. I almost fell into the cockpit when my blind feet stepped backward. Then I was down to the last flying triangle of sail beating Dylan in the face. I grabbed it and pulled. It ripped completely off. It streaked out from my hand and disappeared into the sea.

The sail was quiet. I turned to Dylan. He pointed toward the companionway where we had forgotten to replace the hatch boards. I looked.

The cockpit was still awash from the last wave. Whirlpools spiraled down the scupper holes where the water drained out. As the boat slid down the back of another wave, the water in the cockpit sloshed through the companionway opening. The cabin sole was wet. Gerry lay on the sole with a cushion wedged on either side of him. He was not rolling. He was not crying. His eyes were closed and his arms were crossed over his chest, over Blankie and the red life jacket he had put on all alone in the wet, dark boat.

CHAPTER TWENTY-SIX

I LOOKED AT GERRY for a moment and thought about going down to say something. But I didn't know what to say, and I figured if he was in his roly-poly mode, I would just break his concentration. I hoped he was doing that. Otherwise I didn't know how you could stand to be barely six years old, terrified of the water, and believing you were about to be thrown into the worst water you'd ever seen in your life.

So I crawled back to take the tiller from Dylan and sent him down below.

"Dry off," I yelled in his ear. "Feed yourselves."

I settled back to the helm. Now we were running bare poled before the wind, the hull alone giving the wind enough surface to push us flying across the seas.

Usually when you're steering a boat, it's like steering a

car—you aim yourself in the right direction and move the tiller a little this way or that way to keep on course. Occasionally a stronger puff of wind or a sudden wave pushes you off—like a bump in the road or a car that swings too far into your lane. But you correct. You get back on course. And you start again with the little movements. It's easy. Anyone can do it.

But this tiller was a raging dog I had to hold at heel. We swung wildly from side to side as the waves lifted the boat and twisted it to one side. I pulled the tiller toward me with all my strength, leaning back to get out of the way so I could pull it more and more toward starboard. Then the waves dropped us and twisted us the other way and I was shoving the tiller to port. Away from me. Hard. Hard. As far as it would go. Then we rolled up the back of a wave and were dropped again, maybe this time in the other direction. Maybe not. The compass needle swung through eighty degrees with each wave as I fought to keep our stern to the wind and waves, to keep the boat afloat.

The wind kept shoving us over the waves and shrieking in my ears. The rain kept pummeling me with wet and cold and pounding on my face. The waves kept rising up under us, crashing on top of us, and washing over us. Still we rode on. And on. And on. The day slipped into night. The night slid away, and it was day again. I'd been at the helm for almost twenty-four hours. I hadn't eaten or drunk. I hadn't rested.

As the new day began to lessen the darkness, I realized the rain had almost stopped and the wind was less. It was still stronger than any I'd ever sailed in before, but it was less than it had been. I began to notice my body again, but it was as if it were someone else's. I couldn't change any of the things that were wrong. I was still a human machine acting as an extension of the rudder.

Even so, a piece of my insides unwound enough to think, and I wondered if maybe Dylan had been on the radio this whole time. Maybe rescuers were out there waiting for the storm to calm down enough so they could come and get us. But where would we say we were? We didn't know where we'd started from, and now we'd traveled more than twenty-four hours in a basically southerly direction at an average speed of at least eight knots. Wherever we were, we were definitely a long way from wherever we started.

After a while I saw the hatch boards begin to move. The top one wiggled out and I saw Dylan. He took out the rest of the boards and then crawled out on deck with me. In his foul weather gear he looked like a yellow caterpillar easing through the companionway and clinging to the slanting deck as he crept to my side.

He sat right next to me—bone to bone—and yelled in my ear, "It's my turn."

I looked down at him. Dylan didn't have Gerry's shock of blond hair. His hair was a brownish color. It was too long, of course, and it hung down his neck and over his forehead in wet points. He reached out for the tiller and I saw that his hand was bigger than I remembered. When I didn't let go, he tried to push my hand away.

"You're not strong enough," I screamed, and suddenly had to shove the tiller way to the other side of the boat. Dylan lost his balance and tumbled onto the cockpit floor. I watched the yellow heap sort itself back into arms and legs and he stood again.

"You're not, either—anymore," he yelled back at me. His eyes were so intense and sad. Just looking at them made me feel a little scared.

"I can do it!" I shouted.

"So can I. You're tired."

He put his hand on mine again and pushed. This time my fingers let go their grip. When they moved they hurt. Tears started in my eyes. The boat took a wave too much on the side and suddenly heeled hard to starboard. I fell against a winch and Dylan pulled the tiller tight up against him. Slowly the bow turned south again. We didn't have as much speed without the screaming wind. Steering was going to be different.

"What's the course?" Dylan was staring at the compass.

"No course. Just keep the stern to the waves. That's been roughly south, but we're swinging through eighty degrees."

He didn't look at me. He just nodded once, peered deeply into the compass, and shoved the tiller away from him as he felt the bow swinging around.

He was doing it by feel, exactly the way he should. I rubbed my ribs where the winch had gotten me. A wave dumped a couple of bathtubs of water on top of us, and for the first time since the storm began, I stood and looked aft out across the ocean.

There was enough light now to see, and the sight sent

shock waves through me. We were in the trough of a wave. I was staring into a wall of water. I looked up for the top of the waves. I kept looking. I craned my head backwards.

Forty feet? But I was afraid of exaggerating. Thirty feet at least. Three stories of water, topped by blowing spray, rolled like a moving wall toward the boat. At the bottom of the trough we almost stalled for a moment because the wall blocked the wind. But our momentum from our slide down the front of that monster kept us moving. The rudder still worked. We could still steer. We rose up again to the top of the waves.

The stern began rising first as the wave rolled under us. Then the bow. And by some miracle, the whole massive wall slid underneath us, and we were riding on top of its broad smooth back.

I looked at Dylan. He was like I had been, totally focused on the tiller. He was not conscious of anything around him except keeping our stern facing the waves.

I looked aft again. As far into the gloom as I could see were more waves rolling like an army convoy toward us. One behind the other, each exactly the same, each huge, each mindless, each deadly. How did they get so big while I was watching the compass? Where were they coming from? How long would they go on?

Dylan glanced up at me quickly. "Go down below," he ordered. "You're tired. We need you to rest."

Dylan had already seen the waves. He had seen them hours ago when the sail exploded. He had seen them just now when he came up and insisted on taking the tiller. He knew about them and he wasn't scared.

I had looked at Dylan practically every day of my life. I knew what he looked like. But sitting there like that, a little blob of yellow holding on to a tiller while thirty-foot waves broke on top of him, slinging the water out of his eyes and peering into the compass, suddenly Dylan looked different to me. I went down below.

Gerry was still wedged between the cushions on the floor. I knelt close to his head. He opened his eyes. "I went pee," he said. "Right here on the floor."

"It's okay, buddy," I said. "We all have." I looked down at him. His eyes were pools of darkness in the half-light, but his lips were outlined clearly and the white of his teeth showed between them. The teeth were all still baby teeth. I saw he had bruises on his face. "You're hurt."

He nodded. "I fell off the bunk—a long time ago."

I nodded back, then lay down beside him, the top of my head just touching his. I could feel his warmth and hear him breathing.

"Has Dylan been on the radio?" I asked.

He shook his head. "He tried. It didn't work."

I closed my eyes.

"What about Dad?" he asked.

"Go back to sleep," I said, and then my body and my brain turned off. Dylan was right. I wasn't strong enough. Not anymore.

CHAPTER TWENTY-SEVEN

WHEN I WOKE up, I realized I had made another mistake. I might have slept longer if I hadn't done it, but I had forgotten to put the hatch boards back in when I came below. Water came flying through the companionway and dumped on my head, just like somebody throwing a bucket of water right at me. I felt the water squishing down into my clothes under my foul weather gear. Then the boat shifted and the water rolled back across the cabin floor and into my face again. I lifted up my head and looked around.

The inside of the boat was a little lighter. Everything loose was on the floor. Cans of food were rolling around. Books were lying open, wet and flapping. Dad's charts were pushed up into a corner in a wet heap. As I watched, the sea lifted us high on the starboard side and all the water sloshing on the floor rolled to port. Something plastic swirled around on top. Some of Gerry's little cars flew from the starboard bunk where they had landed in some earlier twist of the boat. They crashed on Gerry's legs where he lay on the floor, his eyes still closed, his arms still crossed over his chest.

I pulled myself back to sit, but it hurt. My ribs were especially sore where I had crashed into the winch, and my left arm felt weak from the time I had spent gripping the boom to tie down the sail. The elbow and wrist ached even when I didn't move.

The boat rose up the front of a wave passing under our stern. Our bow pointed down sharply and everything rolled forward. I reached out and grabbed a can before it rolled into Gerry's head.

I was thinking very slowly, trying hard to be careful but not really awake. I set the can upright, wedged on the floor so that it could not roll from aft to forward again. The boat leveled out on the top of the wave. The wind hit us and raced through the open hole of the companionway. The books fluttered like scared birds, but the charts didn't move. They were a soaked mass of useless paper now.

Then the wave began to move out from under us. The bow tilted up, the stern fell back, and we slid down the wave's back. The can fell over and rolled aft. I came awake completely. There was no such thing as safely wedged in this boat. I felt the boat stall in the trough, and another load of water rushed through the companionway.

I stood and looked at Dylan framed in the companionway opening. He was a yellow spot against a vertical background of black, curling water. The runoff from the last wave was still rolling off his shoulders. He was squinting against the wet and salt in his eyes. One hand clutched the tiller, the other held fast to the rail. The boat yawed in the trough, and he worked with the tiller to keep the boat's stern to the waves. He glanced back for one second to see the next wave coming. The stern began to rise. He looked forward again and saw me standing in the companionway watching.

I came up and out into the storm again.

The sky was lighter and the rain had stopped completely, but the wind was still fierce. When I came topsides, I could hear it howling. It slapped me in the face and pressed against my foul weather gear. It swept my hair back away from my forehead and flung spray into my face, burning my eyes with the wet and the salt.

Then we began to slide down into another trough and the wind eased. Suddenly, I could hear. I sat down beside Dylan. He turned and looked at me, and I saw that he wasn't an eleven-year-old boy anymore. He was an eleven-year-old man. I reached for the tiller.

"I can go longer," he said.

"Don't exhaust yourself," I said. I reached up and pushed the points of hair away from his forehead. Then the top of a wave dropped on us. When it rolled away, his hair was plastered down on his forehead again and water was dripping off the end of his nose. I pushed his hand off the tiller and took over the helm. "Try the radio," I told him.

"I already did," he said. "It's not working."

"Why not?"

He shrugged. "Same problem. I can hear other people, but they can't hear me."

"What do they say?"

"Get to a safe port."

We sat together for a minute. "Go below," I finally said. "Eat something. Drink. Take care of Gerry. Come spell me again in a few hours. We'll take turns."

In the eerie quiet of the trough, I could hear his voice talking to Gerry as he slid the hatch boards into the companionway opening.

Then I was alone again with the waves and wind. The sun was still high somewhere behind the thick cloud cover—it must have been early afternoon now of the second day—but here on the ocean, the light was dim and there was a new rhythm for me to learn. The race across the top of the waves, the foaming wake, the flying spray, the pull of the rudder against the tiller. Then everything getting slower and slower, quieter and quieter, as we slid down into the windless vacuum of the trough, yawing dangerously at the bottom before slowly climbing up to the top once more.

The light was beginning to fade toward night when my brain moved and I decided the wind was lighter. Maybe there wasn't even as much spray. Maybe the waves would get shorter soon. Maybe when things were calm I could fix the radio. Probably just one little wire loose or something. Then we could call for help. Maybe we were just a few miles off an island. Maybe all this was almost over.

I was letting myself come back to life and it wasn't feeling good. I hadn't remembered anything since the storm started. Not Dad or the Bahamas or Mom. For a tiny second, they all glinted through a crack in my consciousness. Then the crack closed as I realized less wind meant we had a whole new set of problems. Now we weren't moving fast enough.

We struggled up the next wave like a tired climber. Then the wind caught our stern and pushed us forward. We rested at the top a moment then began to slide down. At the bottom of the trough, we slowed almost to a stop. The boat yawed to starboard, and we didn't have enough momentum for me to bring her back on course. We were turning sideways to the wall of water behind us. I pushed the tiller back and forth as hard as I could to create forward motion. The starboard swing slowly corrected and we rose up the back of the next wave pointing more south than southeast. The wind took us at the top and we straightened out. It was a hard puff, and it took us safely down and up again.

Okay, I was thinking. *What now?* My heart was racing. How many more dead troughs could we get through? Going forward to hank on a sail would be suicide. And the wind on the wave crests was still too much for *Chrysalis* to handle.

Then I remembered—the engine! Of course. All I had to do was get the engine going and we could easily ride through the troughs and wouldn't be overpowered on the crests. My fingers felt for the little silver toggle switch. It was smooth and cool, just like all those times we anchored. I touched the controls gently and lightly with my fingertips. The engine chugged. It turned over. It caught. I adjusted the rpms and listened. It was a beautiful sound, rhythmic, deep, and steady. It filled my ears and replaced the wild noise of the wind and waves.

And my plan worked. We moved straight through the next trough and up again. I settled the compass into a course that was roughly south. I think I was smiling when Dylan started pulling out the hatch boards again.

He sat beside me but didn't take the tiller right away. He looked out on the ocean. I looked up at the sky. It would have been nice to see the stars starting to come out. It would have been nice to hear Dylan droning on about this one and that one. He pushed my hand off the tiller.

"Less wind," he said.

I nodded.

"South?" he asked.

"Stern to the waves. If they change, we change."

I sat for another minute.

"Go below," Dylan said.

"Anything changes. Anything at all——"

He nodded.

I went below, carefully replacing the hatch boards this time. I pulled off my foul weather gear. I drank water. I ate cheese. I checked over my bruises. I tried the radio. Then I lay down on the floor next to Gerry and slept.

This time I woke up when I felt my head lift slightly off the cabin sole and bang down again. My ear hurt. The engine was chugging away. It was pitch-black in the cabin. I sat up. The movement of the boat had changed and instantly I understood why.

The waves were shorter and closer together. When we traveled to the top of one, we didn't have time to slide into the trough. We crashed down into it, then plowed immediately up the back of the next wave, then slammed down into the next trough. The waves were shorter because the wind had been lighter now for hours. They were closer together because the water was shallower. Wherever we were, we were closer to land that we had been before.

I stood up. I slid the hatch boards out and felt the rush of fresh air. It was so dark outside, I couldn't see Dylan. "Dylan?" I called.

"Hold on!" he yelled. "Here it comes!"

I was standing on the companionway ladder, holding on to the rails. I felt the boat fly off the top of the wave. I bent my knees to break the jolt, waiting for us to crash against the hard surface of the water. Still we went up. We flew.

Then we began to fall.

"Hold—" Dylan started again, then we hit. My knees buckled. My fingers tore away from the handholds. I fell backwards into the cabin. My head slammed against the navigation table and then the floor. Complete dark swallowed me, and all I heard was the vacuum rush of air in outer space. I saw the stars and then I saw and heard nothing.

CHAPTER TWENTY-EIGHT

WHAT HAPPENED NEXT is so confused and crazy that I can't really tell it in a true way. Maybe it is because I got knocked out that I only remember snatches like pieces of a dream. Maybe it is because things really happened that way—in jerks and flashes. Everything completely dark and rushed like a roller coaster through a tunnel, and then everything all brilliant and frozen as if a searchlight were fixed on us.

I woke up hearing Dylan's voice screaming and feeling Gerry poking me in the sore place on my ribs. Then I knew it was Gerry who was doing the screaming at me. Dylan was yelling at Gerry, "What happened! What happened?" And when I realized the engine noise was gone, I realized that actually Dylan was asking about the engine, not about me. He didn't even know about me. I reached out and shoved Gerry away.

"Stop that!" I yelled. "It hurts. I can't think."

Engine gone. No engine. Maybe Dylan killed it on purpose. I staggered up the companionway into the cockpit feeling dizzy and sick.

"Engine?" I asked.

"It died." Dylan's voice was tight. He was scared.

The waves bashed the boat. We were almost sideways to them with no headway. "Stern to the waves!" I yelled.

"How?" Dylan yelled back.

We were swept up a wave and then dropped like a rock into the trough. My knees collapsed under me and I sprawled in the cockpit.

"I'll check the engine," I yelled at Dylan, and somehow made my way back down below. To get to the engine I had to lift away the companionway ladder. The wooden panel behind it could be removed to expose the engine compartment. Just that first step in the tossing boat took precision planning, starting with where to put the loose ladder once I got it off. Then I crawled into the compartment as much as I could—only my head and shoulders, really. The problem, it turned out, was simple. There was air—or water—in the line, just like when we were crossing the Bank. I bled it off and crawled out. Thumbs-up to Dylan, and he started the engine again. I lifted the panel to cover the engine hatch and the engine died again.

Back into the hole. Bleed it again. Out of the hole. Thumbs-up. Dylan starts it. Good sound. It dies. Back into the hole. Throw up into the bilge. Bleed it again. Cut my hand on a wing nut. Out of the hole. Thumbs-up. Dylan starts it. The sound is beautiful. It keeps going. It doesn't skip or race. It purrs. And then it stops.

God, I'm thinking, *we've got water in the fuel tanks.* All that banging and slamming. We knew something would give. The tanks themselves? The seals at the throat? A loose connection in the engine? I crouch to go in again. What else can I do?

We slam into the trough of the waves and the bow swings to starboard as the force of the wave pushes the stern forward. We're sideways to the waves. I can feel us going over. Green water is pouring in the dorade vents on the port side. I wonder where Gerry is. I am holding myself rigid in the square opening to the engine compartment.

Then we are upright again. We didn't broach. *Bleed the engine,* I think. I reach for the nut. The diesel fumes sicken me and I puke again. This time right on my own hands. I feel us suspended in air, then falling.

We smash onto something not water. Something hard. The bottom. Rock. We're aground. The wave slams us again and we float off.

Gerry is on his knees looking at the cabin sole under the navigation table. Water is oozing up through the planks.

We slam again. What's under us? What's out there?

It's dark. The waves are wild.

We're going to sink, I think, and grab Gerry and throw him into the cockpit.

I hoist myself through the companionway and crawl to the

dinghy lashed to the cabin roof. I'm picking at the lines. *Chrysa-lis* slams off a wave. My grip slips. The dinghy balances a moment and then begins to slide uncontrolled toward the water. Suddenly Dylan is there too, grabbing the lines with me as they snake toward the sea, and we are crawling to the cockpit. We lash the dinghy off the stern, blinded as the waves crash over us. Holding our breath. Eyes stinging. Gerry at the helm. Blankie clutched between his knees. Throwing himself against the tiller. Pulling and straining. His face rigid with concentration.

But it didn't matter. There was no such thing as steering *Chrysalis* anymore.

Time stopped and we waited.

All my senses stretched to read the ocean before us.

Where were the coral heads? The rocks? The shoals? My ears strained for the sound of breakers on a beach. My eyes searched for a lighthouse, a marker, or a darker mass that didn't change. Where was the scent of wet sand, of sea grapes or palms, of dead fish caught in the rocks? What was out there? Where were we going?

Then the boat lifted, and the darkness in front of us solidified into a mountain rising out of the water. The waves thrust us up and toward the dark, toward the rocks. And then they dropped us. *Chrysalis* fell square onto a coral head and shuddered from her keel to the tip of her mast. We collapsed like cloth dolls onto the cockpit floor.

Chrysalis pitched forward off the rock, but the waves were not done. They caught us before the bow buried itself underwater and then lifted us again, higher and closer to land. The smell of wet rock and sand blew at us. The waves took us higher and higher and then slammed us bow first into an open wedge in the rock. The boat screamed as the fiberglass sides scraped against the stone. Our forward motion stopped, but the top of the mast above us swung crazily forward, still moving toward land.

Then it swung aft in a powerful whiplash toward the stern and broke. Four feet above the cabin roof, the shrieking metal separated with the pressure of the wild swing. The whole mast crashed down toward the cockpit, then swung to port and splashed into the ocean, dragging the shrouds across the cockpit and pulling the hull slightly sideways with it.

Then the boat was still.

We lay huddled together in the cockpit. I saw that Gerry was spooned up against my belly and I was covering him with one leg and arm. Dylan was curled up facing us, his arms around his head. He was looking back at me in the sudden stillness.

Now the waves slid against *Chrysalis* the way they slide against a dock. They could no longer move her. They had lifted her too high, and she was wedged in too tight. *Chrysalis* held her ground in the dark. She would never sail again, but she wouldn't sink, either. We were safe for a while. It was time to sleep.

CHAPTER TWENTY-NINE

IT WAS DEEP into the night, but I still was not sleeping. *Chrysalis*'s bow had stayed wedged into the rocks, only scraping occasionally against the coral growing at the foot of the rock standing there in the sea before us. The keel also was jammed into the living coral, but the stern hung over a chasm plunging deep into the water.

The waves had calmed as the hours passed. Now they only licked at the hull and tapped here and there like tiny baby hammers. The dinghy floated just aft, momentarily touching the stern and then drifting away. The wind had softened to a breeze, and the clouds were scudding away, leaving a big round moon to light us up where we huddled on our shattered boat.

Dylan lay on the starboard cockpit seat. The cockpit itself was a snarl of lines, a snake pit. But Dylan had gathered the starboard jib sheet and rolled it into a mound to serve as a pillow. His hair was wet and it stuck out from his head like the leaves of a palm. Still, he slept.

I watched him, wondering how he could do that. How could he lie like that—flat on his back, his lips slightly parted, his breath as easy as if he were back at home with the telescope pointed out the window over the roof of the house next door.

And Gerry. He had slept earlier, using his soaked life jacket for a pillow. Now he sat on the jacket in the corner of the cockpit floor. He held his knees clutched to his chest. His face was buried between his knees. Ropes circled under him and around his feet. His bent head and curled body looked very small in the moonlight. I couldn't see his face, but when he was sitting there like that, his hands looked as small as when he was maybe two. When he was making the discovery that he could open the cabinet doors in my room, take out my models one by one, and pick them apart. Those same hands were holding his knees now, and he was shaking very slightly.

I realized then that I was cold too. I thought of Gerry's chest, where we could count his ribs.

"Are you cold?" I asked.

His head shot up and his eyes looked wet in the moonlight.

He was crying. Now that we were okay, he was crying.

"Stop crying," I said. "You'll wake Dylan."

Then the boat lurched slightly when a bigger wave than usual lifted the stern and set us an inch or two higher into the rocks.

Gerry looked out at the sea. "Do you think we're going to sink?"

"I don't know."

"Can I stand up?"

"Suit yourself."

He unfolded himself and shook his feet out of the lines. "I'm cold," he said. "I need Blankie."

"You dropped it on the stern when you were steering. Besides, it's wet. I'll get something else down below."

The mast lay a little across the companionway. The shrouds and halyards made a spiderweb across the opening. I pushed them away and eased into the cabin. Mom used to say our room looked like a tornado had hit it. I wonder what she would have said if she could have seen that cabin. Anything that could break had broken. All the electronics were lying on the floor with little pieces scattered around. Everything was wet. I made my way to the V-berth locker and found two blankets that were half dry. I hugged them to my chest and turned to go back on deck.

I could see Gerry then, silhouetted against the night sky, standing on the stern. I saw him reaching down for Blankie. He was cold. He was scared. He leaned even farther.

Then he was gone and there was a splash and the stern was empty.

I don't remember crossing the cockpit or screaming his name, but Dylan says I stepped on him and woke him and then fell over him screaming.

I do remember standing on the stern, looking into the inky black water that seemed solid like onyx as it reflected back the moon and hid the depths below.

I remember the feel of the water hitting me as I jumped in and Dylan calling my name. Then I descended into blackness as the water closed over my head. I was blind. The boat, the dinghy, the moon, the rocks, the coral, everything disappeared and all I heard was the strange, echoing gurgle the water made running past the dinghy and the slap of the dinghy towline on the ocean surface.

I reached out into the liquid black, knowing that I would hit the rocks soon, that I would scrape and cut against the coral, expecting the stab of the sea urchin spines.

But there was silk. Corn silk floated through my hands and I slowly closed my fingers. Too late. It was gone and I knew it had been Gerry's hair.

My lungs were hurting. I imagined the red bubbles in them exploding and my lungs filling with blood.

My hands pushed me down deeper into the black and I reached again. And again. With my hands, my feet, my toes. My body searched the blackness around me. Then the silk passed me again. Like the air, it was a breeze glancing against my thigh. I grabbed. I got a handful of silk and pulled. Then I got his arm. I felt the T-shirt drifting around his chest and the muscle and bone of his shoulder. I dragged him toward me and locked him under my arm and pulled us up.

The red bubbles were bursting in my eyes now, and the blackness was thick over our heads. Then I heard the dinghy again and that slapping towline and then the lightening circle above me solidified into the moon and then Gerry's head and mine were up out of the water and Dylan was screaming our names over the stern.

I grabbed the line Dylan threw me. I handed Gerry up. Dylan dragged him on board. Still clutched in Gerry's hand was Blankie.

How I found Gerry, I don't know. How he survived, I don't ask. We poured water out of him, actually holding him upside down. Dylan breathed air back into him, and when he stirred, Dylan wrung out Blankie and held it next to his face. Dylan talked to him and hugged him and found the blankets where I had dropped them. He wrapped up Gerry and then turned and tucked one around me.

All this time, I just watched. I sat on the cockpit floor, clutching my knees to my chest, shivering and watching. Then when Dylan had wrapped us up and Gerry was still and sleeping, I realized that the salt water on my face was warm and the sobs I was hearing were mine.

THE ISLAND

CHAPTER THIRTY

THE THING ABOUT life is that it goes on. You wake up and there is the sun like always. There is your own body with bad breath and bruises and a headache. You have to move. You have to pee. You have to get a drink. No matter what happened the day before, you wake up and there is life and you have to do something about it.

When I woke up that day, I was lying on the cockpit floor in a snarl of hard lines. One was pressing into the sore place on my ribs. The floor hurt my bruised skull. My hands felt cramped and stiff. My mouth was dry.

Gerry shifted quietly where he was sitting above me on the cockpit seat. A corner of Blankie slipped down and tickled my face. He snatched it back up and looked down at me. Our eyes locked, but we didn't say anything or even smile. Dylan sat quietly on the stern, gazing into the gently moving water, his hand resting lightly on the tiller.

I sat up slowly, clearing a place in the boat rubble left by the storm. As my hand passed over the textured fiberglass, I thought how cool it was, how white, how perfect. My mind flashed to the cabin and I remembered the seepage under the sole after our first strike. I leaned into the open hatch to look. The cabin was six inches deep in seawater.

I sat back a moment and closed my eyes. I was tired. I wanted someone to give me a glass of water or to make me take a shower and put on clean clothes.

"We'd better start loading the dinghy," I said.

Dylan turned to look at me, then stood.

Gerry didn't move. "Where are we going?" he asked.

I looked around. It was a fair question.

Chrysalis was wedged about a hundred yards east of a small island. Eight jagged rocks broke the surface of the water around us. They rose up from the seaward edge of an underwater, coral-studded cliff that fell straight down into the ocean below her stern. Between the island and the rough semicircle of rocks lay a bed of coral just under the water's surface. Closer to land, waves broke on a tumble of rocks fallen from the cliff. No beach softened the edge. There were only the rocks in the ocean and the rough, low cliffs that looked as if they were still crumbling day by day into the sea.

The island sloped down on the northern end to a long point that disappeared into the water. It must have continued just under the surface for several hundred yards because breakers were crashing far out from the island on that end. To the south, the island cliffs turned a sudden curve and disappeared.

All around us in a brilliant circle for hundreds and thousands of empty miles, we could see only the moving, glittering ocean and that one island with no beach to land on.

It was a fair question. Where *were* we going?

"I don't know," I said. "But we have to go somewhere."

Chrysalis's bow was forced slightly up so that at the forepeak a foot of her bottom paint showed above the water. The stern was forced down so that the taller waves splashed gently over the toe rail. The strain of the mast hanging over the side pulled her deeply to port. The falling mast had opened holes in the hull and left a gash in the deck just aft of the foresail winch. We couldn't see what was wrong underneath. All we knew was that the cabin was slowly filling with water. Steadily the water's weight and the dragging mast would pull *Chrysalis* toward the chasm under her stern. Someday she would slide backwards and sink completely and irrevocably to the bottom of the sea.

We didn't want to be on *Chrysalis* when that happened. Life was still going on whether we liked it or not, and it was time to load the dinghy. Water, food, dry matches, can opener, blankets, dishes. The dinghy was small. We couldn't fit much. The dinghy motor was still safely stowed in the cockpit locker. The gasoline can was still lashed to the stern. I bolted on the motor and filled the tank while Dylan and Gerry loaded the cargo. They climbed in, Dylan untied the towline, and I slowly backed away.

I headed north, figuring this island was like all the others we had seen—on the inner curve of the crescent, we would find a beach where we could land. Since the island seemed to slope to the north, that seemed the obvious direction to go.

We went slowly. The waves were still too high for an easy dinghy ride, but they were nothing after the waves of the storm. We traveled straight into them, plowing up their fronts and splashing down their backs. The gear in the bottom of the boat shifted and slid, but nobody moved. We just sat and stared at the island on our left while we slowly neared the point where it melted into the sea.

As the dinghy's bow edged past the rise, we were all straining to see what was hidden behind the mound of land, but all we saw was another coral reef stretching toward the west and the line of the island disappearing toward the south. If there was a beach to be found, it would have to be on the western side of the island. I turned my gaze now toward the breakers on our left and concentrated on taking the dinghy past them. Another hundred yards north and we would leave them safely astern. We could turn west and skirt the northern edge of the coral reef.

A can of chili rolled over my toes just as Dylan sucked in his breath. He closed his eyes slowly and then opened them. Gerry held Blankie clutched over the bottom half of his face.

His eyes relaxed. They were looking back toward the island, paying no attention at all to the breakers. I turned and looked over my shoulder.

Unrolling into view was the tip of a beach lying on the southern end of the western side of the island. As we passed the breakers and turned west, the whole of the beach slowly appeared. It was perfect—a wide, white curve of sand protected on the south and east by the island itself and on the north by the return curve of the island and the long spit of sand just under the surface. A calm, turquoise pool edged the beach, and farther out lay the darker shadows of a coral reef, protecting the western exposure but far enough below the surface for the dinghy to pass over. Behind the beach stood a band of the usual scrub bushes and trees. But on this island, the vegetation then rose up steeply, climbing a tall hill that formed the bulk of the landmass and that, in the still early morning, threw a shadow across the innermost curve of the beach.

We threaded the dinghy carefully through the coral and puttered slowly over the crystal inner water, watching our own shadow move across the sandy bottom. Then we landed gently, leaving a gouge in the flawless sand as we pulled the dinghy high above the tide line. We sat close together in the shade of a clump of sea grapes. Gerry wrapped Blankie around his shoulders. Dylan picked up a dried-up berry and tried to squeeze it. I dug my toes in the sand and watched a seagull wheeling and cawing in the sky while a tern plunged for the kill.

I closed my eyes and tried on words. *Safe. Lonely.* They fit pretty well. *Beautiful* was good. And *quiet.* I lay back in the sand. It was warm. It was solid. I didn't ever want to leave.

But I had to. I stood. "Come on," I said. "Let's unload. Then I'll go get more."

On my first trip, I took off the sails, all the lines, and the tool kit. The next time I got the spinnaker pole to help hold up the tent we planned, the first-aid kit, the speargun, the fishing tackle, and everything else out of the cockpit lockers. On the third trip, I stripped the cabin of everything useful and then wedged our shoes and clothes into the gaps under the seats.

When we had unloaded all the stuff, Dylan showed me where they had laid out the cans of food and water bottles for counting. It didn't look like much. "I should get the water from *Chrysalis*," I said, and Dylan nodded.

I was tired, but I went back. It took a while to figure out what to put the water into, but eventually I found a box of trash bags. I doubled them and put about a gallon of water in each. I tied the bags tightly and propped them carefully in the dinghy so they wouldn't roll over. On the eleventh bag, the water tank ran dry. I pulled out all the plastic tubing that ran from the tank to the sinks and shower, because Dylan had said we could use it. I found a roll of paper towels and another stash of food—five cans of fruit and an unopened loaf of bread. This time I was sure nothing important was left on the boat, and it was time to build our camp.

Dylan and Gerry had picked a spot on the edge of the

beach just under the shade of the scrub trees. They had cleared away the big debris and stacked our stuff in neat piles. We worked together to build the tent. We lashed the three corners of the number one genoa to some low bushes and used the spinnaker pole to prop up the middle of the long, straight side. It made a nice big tent, closed in on three sides but open to the beach. We were a little unprotected that way, but somehow we all wanted to see out over the ocean.

Inside the tent we brushed the floor clean down to the bare sand. We used some life jackets as pillows. We stashed some of the supplies in the very back of the tent and spread the jib over the others outside. We brushed another area clean for the water, spread a blanket over the spot, and carefully placed the bags so they supported one another. Then we covered it all with another blanket weighted all the way around with sand.

The last thing we did on that very first day was to put out our signal for help. Dylan and I knew what we were doing, but we didn't explain it to Gerry. We told him we needed more shade. We rigged the spinnaker high in the trees so that it cast a large triangle of shade in the afternoon sun. From the sky, the bright blues and pinks of the sail would be moving and waving like a giant signal flag to anyone who flew over.

When night started coming, we built a fire and heated a can of chili. We each took a spoon and ate straight out of the can. When we finished, we heated another. It was the best chili we ever ate. We watched our fire burn down to nothing and then lay down inside the tent. Beside me Gerry wrapped Blankie around his neck and curled up with his mouth slightly open. Across the tent, Dylan lay still, his breath coming evenly in the dark.

The silence rolled in on me and the tent got way too small. My mind started replaying the storm, and when I heard the mainsail explode, I stood and walked out into the night. For a while I sat under the spinnaker and listened to the gentle rustle as it moved in the breeze. Then I walked down to the beach.

The wind there was strong enough to tickle the hair on my arms, but not so strong that it drowned out the sounds of the island. I could hear the hiss of the tiny nighttime waves dying on the shore and the clack and rattle of sea grape and palm leaves in the brush. The moon that had reflected off the water last night had not yet risen. The island was a black shadow behind me, and the waves an invisible mystery before me.

I lay on the sand just beyond the reach of the little waves and tried on words again, but now nothing fit. I looked up at the sky filled with stars and tried to feel wonder, but I felt nothing.

I thought that it was possible at a time like that to cry. There was a switch inside somewhere, and a person could just decide to flip it and start crying. Maybe it looked and felt like the toggle switch on the engine. Silver and smooth. One direction was on; the other direction was off. Easy to flip. You do it without looking. Up—you're happy and strong. Down—you're crying and weak.

I couldn't remember having cried for years—until last night when Gerry had almost drowned. Tonight, the world was quiet and my brothers were sleeping safely. But I was alone and I was looking at tomorrow—and the next day and the next day and the next day.

My mind fingered the silver switch. To dissolve in crying, to wade out into the dark ocean, to disappear into deep space. My insides trembled. I stood and walked partway down the beach and then back again. I pressed my fingers against my eyes. I stretched my arms high toward the stars, my fingers spread across the sky.

"'Rage,'" I said to the wind, my voice tight in my throat. "'Rage against the dying of the light.'"

The moon tipped the summit of our island and within minutes I was standing in a pool of silver light. At my feet the curling edges of the waves glittered with the fractured shards of the moon's reflection.

I turned and went back to the tent. Dylan was sitting up. "You couldn't sleep?" he asked.

"No," I said, "but I'll be okay now." And I was.

CHAPTER THIRTY-ONE

WE RESTED FOR almost a week, mostly sleeping. When we moved, it was to eat or drink or tie something tighter. We never left our beach. On the sixth day, we decided to go back to scour the boat for anything else we could use. Dylan hoped that with the sextant he could figure out where we were, and Gerry wanted his little cars. The wind was coming at about fifteen knots out of the north, perfect for a boat like *Chrysalis*, but hard in the dinghy. As we crossed the coral reef and rounded the northern point of the island, we saw *Chrysalis*. She was still there, but her stern had sunk noticeably deeper.

I guided the dinghy to her leeward side, carefully puttering around the fallen mast. When Dylan had snagged a cleat with the towline, we all just sat and looked at the wreck. Seagulls had left their droppings all over the deck. The movement of the loosened shrouds had left scratches, now filling with dirt and mold. The shredded mainsail was rotting in the sun.

This *Chrysalis* was very different from the one I still had in my mind. I remembered leaving Florida on her. I had hated her. Then I swam under her on the Great Bahama Bank and I saw her complete in the water—her dark, round underneath, her shining sides, her sail wings. In the storm, I felt her struggle—the climb up the waves, the strain on the tiller, the tremble of the rudder. She was strong and beautiful. She had carried us safely. And now we were looking at her wreck.

If Gerry had brought Blankie with him, he would have pulled it over his head. Instead, he looked away and back and away again. We had to keep going.

"Gerry, you and I will go first," I said. "Then Dylan, we'll bring up the gear while Gerry watches the dinghy."

Dylan nodded. I climbed on board and gingerly lifted Gerry on after me. Our weight did not affect her set in the water. She was solid. We stepped carefully down the sloping deck into the cockpit and leaned into the companionway. Gerry sat down suddenly and I grabbed him, afraid he was falling.

"Oh, Ben," he said. He spread his hands over his face and refused to look again.

I could see why. Toward the stern, the cabin was more than a foot deep in water. Clothespins and trash floated on the surface where an oil or diesel leak had created a sheen. In a corner of the settee, a black growth spread across the sopping cushions as they soaked up the water lapping at the top of the seats.

I rubbed Gerry's hair. "Buck up, buddy," I said. "I'll get your stuff." I slid down into the water, kicked aside a cushion floating at my knees, and slogged to Gerry's bunk. His books were dry, though they were in a tangled heap from the tossing of the storm. A little drawstring bag underneath held his collection of clothespins, some cars, and shells. When I brought them out to Gerry, he cradled them in his arms and crawled to the dinghy, tears drying on his cheeks.

Dylan, too, was startled at the mess, the trash, the dirtiness of it. It was such an undignified way for *Chrysalis* to slip away. He sloshed to the V-berth and came out carrying his star books and *The Chronicles of Narnia*. He found the sextant still under the lid of the nav table.

I thought about what was in my berth. I didn't want my car magazines. My diesel engine book was useless. Then I remembered Mom. Her picture was still wedged in the book, and though the book was in half an inch of water, she was dry. I slid her into my shirt pocket. She was still smooth and shiny. She was still smiling.

Then I crawled into Dad's bunk. There was nothing there. His mattress was already soaking in the water. I was backing out when I saw his poetry collection. I had left the book on his pillow the morning the storm started. Then the storm had tossed his pillow to port, and the permanent list of the boat had kept it there. The pillow had folded itself halfway around the small, fat book. I could see the book and the edge of the note just sticking out between the pages.

I unfolded the pillow and took out the book. My hand on the book looked like Dad's. It made me dizzy. As I sat on the edge of his bunk, pushing the pillow away, the pillowcase slipped and the corner of something inside showed. I pulled it out.

It was the apron. Mom's apron. The one she always wore. The one she reached around behind her to tie in a bow— without looking. The one in the dark, and Dad sliding down the front of the cabinet, and Gerry crying.

I pressed it hard against my face and breathed deep.

Late at night Mom and Dad were in the kitchen and I came down for a drink. Quietly down the stairs and into the dark hall. They were standing there in the moonlight. Mom had the apron pressed to her face and she was crying. Dad wrapped his arms around her. "Shhh," he said. "It'll be okay. Shush, now." She dropped her arms and pressed her face against his chest. She sobbed and choked when she breathed in. Dad rubbed her back. "Shush, now," he said over and over. "Shush, now, baby. Shush now." She cried, and silently I climbed the stairs again.

I rubbed the apron against my face and breathed it in. Surely her scent lay hidden in the folds. I breathed in again. Over and over. Then I heard Dylan's feet topsides. I picked up the book and stuffed the apron into my waistband.

"Are you coming?" Dylan called.

"One second." I stood at the foot of the companionway ladder and looked around.

It was all so familiar. The little rail that held the books and flashlights on the shelf. The deep blue color of the cushions. The long scratch in the dinette table. The dull silver of the aluminum sink. The things we handled every day and never paid attention to—the handrails, the porthole locks, the light switches. And the things we had thought we couldn't live without—Gerry's little-kid CD player, my car magazines. They were all going to disappear. They were going to sink and rot.

I climbed back into the sunlight where Dylan and Gerry were sitting quietly in the dinghy, waiting for me. I handed Dad's book to Dylan and started the engine. We had skirted the stern and were heading north when I saw Gerry lift his hand and wave. Then Dylan waved too.

I turned to look back. From this distance, her sides were still shining white. She was tilted at a crazy angle and her mast was broken, but she was still beautiful. We rode the waves a few moments watching, but that was all we could do. The wind was picking up and the waves were pounding us. I turned the dinghy north again, rounded the point, and headed across the shallows over the coral toward our beach. Now we were going with the waves, but the dinghy didn't have a keel to keep it straight in the water. We were bouncing around on top of the waves like a cork. The closer we got to the beach, the more the waves became breakers. Dylan and Gerry huddled around our haul trying to keep everything dry. The books had made it through the storm and now here we were just trying to get to the beach and everything was getting soaked.

But I was more worried about beaching us. Normally when you beach a dinghy, you slide in on gentle waves, hop out quickly, and then haul the dinghy up the sand before any waves can knock it around. But these waves were too big. If we had had a choice, I would have said we couldn't land. But we had no choice. We'd just have to do the best we could and get ready for a beating.

Nearer shore, the breakers were bigger and closer together. We would ride over one, and the next one would break on our stern. "You guys are going to have to jump," I told Dylan and Gerry. "Just jump in and wade to the beach when I say go."

"I can't," Gerry said.

"But when I beach it, I'll have to kill the engine and tilt it up to keep it from dragging in the sand. I'll lose control of the boat. You guys have to be out before then."

Dylan nodded. He took Gerry's arm.

"No!" Gerry cried, and clutched his books and toys.

"Now!" I shouted.

As Dylan lifted Gerry, threw him over, and jumped out after him, I spun the boat away and headed straight back out into the breakers. When I turned back toward shore, Dylan was dragging Gerry through the water. Their hands were empty and Gerry was crying, but they were safe on the beach. Nobody hurt—yet.

My turn. I planned to take the boat in as close as I could,

then kill the engine and tilt it up so the prop wouldn't bang into the sand. Without the prop, I had no way to steer. I'd just have to ride the waves in. If I was lucky, I'd ride all the way in and hardly wet a toe getting out. If I was unlucky, the waves would turn the dinghy upside down and it would beat me to death.

I kept the speed up going toward the beach so I could control the boat through the breakers. I was watching carefully, trying to gauge the depth of the water and how close I could get, but today the bottom was blurred with stirred-up sand. I tried to remember the slope of the bottom. I tried to measure distance by the size of Gerry and Dylan standing on the beach watching me. I was concentrating. I was careful. But I waited too long.

Just as I was reaching for the button to kill the engine, I felt it. The dinghy fell straight down. The prop slammed into the sand, grabbing it and holding the dinghy momentarily like an anchor. The motor twisted on the stern. A breaker rolled over the top of the motor and poured into the bottom of the dinghy. Then the dinghy rose up. The motor twisted the opposite way and fell off, disappearing into the waves. The dinghy bobbed free, but heavy. I grabbed the starboard side to throw myself into the water when another breaker hit and shoved the dinghy portside down into the waves. I fell out backwards, splashing uncontrolled into the water. I heard the dinghy inches from my head and furiously pushed against the sand, away from the tremendous rocking weight of the dinghy, now half-submerged and lumbering through the waves toward the beach.

I righted myself in the breakers and stood to see the dinghy already ten feet away washing toward the southern curve of the beach. I spat out sand and wiped my eyes while Dylan and Gerry stood on the beach, watching the dinghy sluggishly bobbing along until it stopped a hundred feet away in six inches of water. The waves drove its bow into the sand and then washed over its stern to fill it deeper and deeper with water.

Finally Dylan moved. He walked slowly to the dinghy, picked up the towline snaking around in the water, and pulled. Of course it didn't move. I sloshed out to join him, but even with both of us it didn't move. Two people cannot drag a dinghy full of water through the sand. Gerry brought us one of the spare lines from our gear. I tied the two lines together, then tied the longer line to a low tree on the edge of the beach. At least now it wouldn't wash away. I could worry about salvage later.

I sat down by Dylan and Gerry and we looked at the dinghy.

"We didn't lose it," I said. "When the tide's down, we'll bail and drag it high on the beach. It'll be okay."

"What about the motor?" Dylan asked.

"Lost," I said. "And ruined."

He nodded.

"The other stuff?" I asked.

"All lost," he said. "And ruined."

I touched my pocket and felt the wet stiffness of Mom's picture. Not lost, I thought. Not ruined.

Then I remembered and felt at my waistband. Gone. I had meant to put it under my pillow. I had meant to breathe it again. To find the scent.

I rested my elbows on my knees and looked down at the sand I was sitting on. Zillions of little grains—white and pink and black. Little broken-up shells and tiny branches of coral. All piled here to make an island. And we were on it. The three of us together. Lost in the middle of the great wide sea.

CHAPTER THIRTY-TWO

WE SPENT MOST of our energy the next day digging the dinghy out of the sand, bailing it, and dragging it high up on the beach. I snorkeled for the engine, but the sand had completely buried it. Nobody could remember what happened to the paddles, but it didn't matter. I told Gerry we could find something to use if we needed to, but I knew we would never get back to *Chrysalis*. Even the coral reef was too far for us now.

In the afternoon we sat under the waving spinnaker and looked out to sea. After a while, Gerry curled up on his side and fell asleep and Dylan wandered away to look at the sea grapes. I was thinking numbers. We had been on the island seven days. We had drunk two of our bags of water and eaten almost half our stash of food. Maybe we were in good shape.

Maybe a plane would fly over tomorrow or a boat would sail up two or three days later. With the spinnaker flying and *Chrysalis* wedged in the rocks, our situation would be obvious to a boat passing on the east or north or to an airplane flying overhead.

Or maybe that wouldn't happen. Maybe no planes ever flew over. Maybe no boats ever passed by. We hadn't seen anything for the last seven days. Unless—

Dylan suddenly sat down beside me. "It's too early," he said. "I don't know when they'll be ready."

"What?"

"The sea grapes. They're edible, you know. People even make jelly out of them. But I don't know when they'll be ready."

I nodded. Then I pointed to Gerry sleeping and whispered, "I want to talk." Dylan quietly followed me down the beach to sit in a patch of shade under a palm.

"Dylan," I said, "we need to see what's on the other side of this island."

He sat a minute, then asked, "What do you think is there?"

"I don't know, but maybe there's another beach—without the coral reef."

I looked at him closely. Dylan never seemed to squint or tighten up his eyes when he was thinking. They weren't especially big eyes, but they were always round and dark. And he had small, neat ears like Mom's. Little ears that barely showed now under his ragged hair. And his hands were still—not fingering the grass or digging in the sand. They were quiet beside him while he looked at me and knew what I meant.

"You mean maybe there's a place on this island where a big boat would actually choose to anchor," he said.

"Yes." I looked out at the water. "Coral reef to the north and west. Cliff and rocks to the east. Apparently cliff to the south. That leaves the southeast."

"Maybe there's a boat there right now," Dylan said.

I nodded. "But how would we know? We have to go see what it's like."

So we decided to explore the rest of the island. On an almost gray day when clouds were scudding overhead and we thought we felt a drop of rain every now and then, we put on the shoes we had brought off *Chrysalis* and packed the last three breakfast bars, a knife, and a jar of water in a shirt tied around my waist.

I made Gerry leave Blankie, so he started the trip crying and dragging behind. Dylan and I were already scrabbling through the rocks at the western tip of the beach while Gerry was still wandering around camp. "Sit down," I told Dylan. "We'll wait here where he can't see us. That'll make him catch up."

We waited and the silence grew. Dylan lifted his head slightly and looked. "He's still dragging that stick in the sand. He hasn't noticed yet."

Then Gerry's voice carried to our hideaway. "Ben? Dylan?"

We didn't answer.

"I wish we had the EPIRB," Dylan said quietly. "It would send a signal."

"Dad sure didn't need it," I said.

"He did need it. I wish we'd had two."

I shook my head. "You have to accept it, Dylan. He drowned himself and left us to die in the storm."

"He didn't know about the storm. The storm came later."

I opened my mouth, then closed it. "Okay," I said. "The storm came later. But he went over on purpose. And he took the thing we need most to get us off this island."

"Dylan! Ben!" This time it was a little more shrill.

"Someone will have found Dad," Dylan said. "And now he'll find us."

"Dylan, be reasonable," I said.

"If there's a boat over there," he continued, "it'll be a lot easier."

"And if there isn't—or if there isn't anywhere for one to anchor? What's the plan then? Just to wait?"

Dylan nodded. "And stay alive," he said.

We sat looking at each other.

"Don't leave me, guys!" Now there was fear in Gerry's voice.

We glanced back toward the sound of Gerry's feet, then stood at the same instant. There was Gerry about twenty feet away, picking his way through the rocks.

He looked up at us and understood we had been hiding.

"That was mean," he said, and lifted a corner of Blankie to cover his mouth.

"You brought Blankie," I said.

He nodded, still holding the corner to his mouth.

"Well, don't lose him. And keep up."

With Gerry right behind me now and Dylan bringing up the rear, we climbed over the pile of rocks at the end of our beach. There we found another, much smaller and very different beach. If any beach could have been more beautiful than ours, this one was. Here the rocks rolled into the water like a low landslide. Right up next to the land was a broken-up sort of beach where sand had sifted in among the fallen rocks. The tide was low now, but we could see from the line of sea wrack where the high water came. Big, bathtub-size rocks lay scattered in the sand and glistened with algae and snail tracks where the water lapped at high tide. Some kind of mussel the size of a marble lived among the smaller rocks where they lay in piles kept damp by the tides. Steps away were tumbled rocks that had captured seawater and held it even at low tide. And beyond that were rocks that lay permanently half underwater with coral beginning to grow on the bumpy surfaces and sea urchins hiding in the crevices.

I closed my eyes and listened. The rocks softened the sound of the waves and blocked the wind. The birds were silent. I could hear Dylan and Gerry breathing beside me and the cuddling move Gerry made to nestle a corner of Blankie against his face.

Then I turned to climb the pile of rocks at the end of the tiny beach. Before the others moved, I could see over. The wind tore at my hair and the roar of the waves filled my ears. I saw that I was standing on the southwestern tip of the island. To my left the island turned sharply back to the east. The wild ocean pounded at the rocks that had broken off the landmass and dropped into the sea. To my right, the landslide of rocks holding the secret beach lay like stepping stones out into the ocean all the way to the coral reef where it turned southward. Along the rocks' seaward side, the water looked deep and still, until it met the pile at my feet. There the waves crashed and turned back on themselves in flying sheets of spray. I climbed back down as Dylan and Gerry waited.

"Can't go that way. Nothing but ocean and rocks. No beach."

Dylan's face clouded.

"Let's go straight up here." I pointed toward the summit. "We'll be able to see the whole island from there and get a better idea."

"A better idea of what?" Gerry asked.

I waited for Dylan to jump in with an answer, but he didn't. "Of how the island's shaped," I said, and charged off toward the trees.

The band of trees lasted for only about ten minutes of climbing. Then we started pushing our way through scrub bushes and cactuses. I was leading the way, trying to find gaps and spaces that weren't there. The clouds overhead were shifting and the sun broke through occasionally, hot and intense.

When I heard a rattle low in the bushes ahead of us, I froze. "Snake!" I whispered.

Gerry stopped instantly just behind me.

"Snake?" Dylan asked, easing up behind Gerry.

"I heard a rattle."

"There aren't any rattlesnakes in the Bahamas—or even any poisonous snakes."

"Are we in the Bahamas, Ben?" Gerry asked.

"I don't know," I said. "Maybe. Probably. I don't know."

"But we're close," Dylan said. "And there are no poisonous snakes here."

"How do you know?"

"I read it."

"And you're sure you remember it right?"

"Yes."

"Sure enough to lead the way?"

"Yes." He started to step forward.

"Never mind. I need you in back to keep Gerry moving."

We started off again. I went a little more slowly. I looked more deeply into the bushes. The sun broke through completely, and my head was instantly hot through my bandanna. I saw no snakes.

"Stop," Dylan said. "There he is."

I felt a hot rush along my back.

"Who?" Gerry asked, and we looked where Dylan was pointing.

An iguana sat sunning on a low rock ten feet farther up the hill.

"There's your snake, Ben," Dylan said.

The iguana was fat, with a body about a foot long and a tail dragging behind him another eighteen inches. He looked more like a dinosaur than a lizard. His leathery skin hung on him in folds. His feet spread out in claws on the hot rock. He waited with his back to us, his eyes staring forward. He blinked.

"Do they bite?" Gerry asked.

"Of course they bite," Dylan said. "But not people."

"He looks like he'd bite," Gerry said.

"Well, don't get close to him," I said. "Let's go."

"Wait," Dylan said, and held up his hand. "Maybe we could catch him."

"Why?" I asked.

"To eat," Dylan said.

I took another step, then I stopped. I looked at Dylan again. "Okay. How do you catch them? Or clean them? Or cook them?"

"I don't know," Dylan said, not shifting his eyes from the iguana.

"Well, that's a lot of help," I said.

"But, Ben," Gerry said. "I'll bet we could figure it out."

"Now? This very minute? In this roasting sun?"

"No." Dylan looked at me. "Let's go on. I need to think about it."

We stepped forward, and the startled iguana hobbled off the rock and into the shadows under the bushes.

I started up the hill again. "Figure it out quick," I said. "I'm getting hungry."

I shouldn't have said that. It made the sun hotter, the land drier, the bushes thornier. When Gerry walked too close to a cactus and got a shower of spines in the back of his hand, we found another rock and sat down. I started pulling the spines out of Gerry's hand while he screamed and tried to yank his hand away. Dylan worked on Blankie, which naturally had dragged through the cactus along with Gerry's hand. When we had done the best we could and Gerry was just sniffing, I took out the jar of water and the breakfast bars. The water was good, but when we bit into the bars, they were stale and tasted moldy. Gerry wanted to spit his out, but I wouldn't let him.

"You've got to eat it," I shouted. "There's nothing else!" I clamped my hand over his mouth. "Swallow!"

He looked up at me with round, drowning eyes, and I was rocked by the memory of Dad holding him underwater at Honeymoon Harbour. I jerked my hand away and watched him let the wet, brown blob roll out of his mouth and drop into the sand.

I covered my eyes. "I'm too tired to keep going," I said. "Let's go back."

"Wait," Dylan said. He picked up the knife and cut off a pear from a prickly pear growing five steps away. He carried the pear gingerly to the rock, scraped off the spines, and sliced it open. He cut out a piece of the red pulp, slid it into his mouth, and started chewing. We watched and waited. He worked hard at swallowing, then shivered a little.

"Not great," he reported, "but it will do."

I held out my hand for a piece, and then Gerry's little hand appeared beside mine, palm up and open. It's funny what you'll do, I thought, when you run out of choices.

And I had to admit that when we were finished I felt better. Maybe it was the handful of calories zooming around in my bloodstream. Maybe it was the way the breeze had come up and was cooling us in spite of the sun. Maybe it was the way the cactus looked different to me now. Anyway, I felt strong enough to keep going, and so did the others. I packed the jar and knife back into the shirt, tied it around my waist, and led the way.

When we reached the top of the island, we felt the wind hit us and push against us, as if it were trying to shove us back down the hill we had just climbed. But we braced ourselves, bending slightly forward and ignoring its roar in our ears. We turned together, like filings reacting to a magnet, and faced the rocks where *Chrysalis* had foundered.

There they were, rising up out of the moving, breaking water. There were the shallows where the colors of the coral were visible even from up here. And then the eight jagged rocks. And then the fathomless blue of the ocean, like the deep blue of space, spreading out toward the horizon and broken in the near distance into a reflective confusion of ridges and hollows where the waves rolled and twisted under the sun.

But there was no *Chrysalis*.

I don't know what I expected to see. Did I think *Chrysalis* would still be there? Did I hope she would? Did I hope at least to see her shape, white and ghostly under the water, or a gouge in the rocks or a shroud still trailing across the shallow coral—anything to prove that she once had been there?

I guess it was the complete blank that opened a hole in my chest and made me feel as if the wind were blowing through me and sucking away my breath. I watched the waves breaking on the rocks and began to forget which rocks were the ones we had hit. They started to shift in my memory, and for a second I panicked. Then I remembered clearly. Those two right there, of course. No others were close enough together to have caught the bow and held it like a vise the way those two had done.

Looking down, I saw that we had been lucky. If the rocks had not caught *Chrysalis*, she would have been dashed onto the shallower coral banks and we would have had to abandon her immediately, launching the dinghy in the dark into the crashing waves. We would have been thrown onto the coral and sliced to pieces. But that didn't happen. We were past that. We were safe on this island. This island, such as it was.

I took a deep breath and looked around.

Now we could see that the island was shaped like a boomerang with the right angle pointing almost due east. The top arm of the boomerang pointed northwesterly except for the tip which curved back due north and then narrowed and sloped into the sea. The bottom arm of the boomerang was much thicker and pointed southwest, ending in the blunt pile of stepping-stone rocks we had just explored. The meeting of the two arms was the highest point, where we now stood.

From here we could see almost every line where the island met water, and now, for the first time, we could see the southeastern shore. Only it wasn't a shore. It was a cliff. Straight down into the ocean with no tumbled rocks or coral reef. Just a sheer drop into the crashing waves. Nothing but a dinghy could ever land on this island, and then only on the single beach where we had built our camp. I looked at Dylan and he looked at me.

Then I looked again at the lonely, breathtaking beauty of where we were. The bushes and trees clung proudly and stubbornly to the thin layer of soil over the rocks. They would not be beautiful anywhere else, but here they were perfect— stunted trees bent by the wind, dull green bushes prickly to the touch, grasses that crunched underfoot, and cactuses stabbing defiantly up at the now cloudless, rainless, infinitely blue sky. And everywhere there were the rocks—the striated wall of the cliffs, the tumble of gigantic boulders, the smaller rocks huddled in the edge of the sea. All a deep, grayed brown mottled with dampness or patches of algae or the shivering slate green of some determined plant growing in a crevice. Around them all lay the pristine beach, the aqua shallows, the ocean-blue deeps, and the sudden, brilliant flashes of colored coral growing silently and steadily under the waves.

And then there were the creatures that lived here. The seagulls and pelicans and hawks and terns screeching through the sky. The iguanas and snakes and lizards and who knew what else scrabbling along in the bushes. The mussels and sea urchins. The crabs and the conch. The tiny fish flashing across the face of the coral. The larger ones hiding in the crevices and slipping through the seaweed. And just on the far side of the coral reef, the big ones—the silent rays, the graceful tuna, and the slender sharks.

I tried on words. *Majestic. Stunning. Awesome.*

Then I looked down at my brothers, standing small beside me. We were three little pieces of humanity, the only people on earth, standing on the very top of the island, erect, on two feet, with hands at our sides. In a photograph or a painting, we wouldn't show up. There was so little of us and so much of everything else.

I was holding Gerry's hand to keep him from stepping too close to the edge. Dylan stood exactly at my other side, not even as high as my shoulder now.

The waves crashed on the rocks. The seagulls cawed and spun on invisible currents in the air. The thin grass hissed slightly in the wind. But we were quiet. Only one word echoed in my mind now. Over and over, pounding like the drumbeat of a dirge.

Despair. Despair. Despair.

CHAPTER THIRTY-THREE

IT WAS ABOUT another week before I let it sink in that we were really going to have to do something about food and water. With careful use, the fresh water left from *Chrysalis* would last a while, but the food would only last another day.

I kept expecting something amazing to happen. Maybe we'd be wandering through the sea grapes and—boom—there would be a fabulous plant that contained all the basic nutrients and tasted good. Or we'd be swimming and suddenly discover an oyster bed or a cache of lobster. Or we'd miraculously develop the ability to catch fish with our bare hands. I must have seen movies like that a hundred times. And all those books— *Swiss Family Robinson*, *Robinson Crusoe*, *The Cay*. People did it that way, I knew. So where was our miracle?

We didn't get one. We just got hungry. We ate the last can

of food for lunch and looked at each other and knew there was not another one in our stash.

I picked up the speargun and waded out into the water. It was absurd. The turquoise pool contained no fish. I knew that. I couldn't swim out to the coral reef and just hang around in the middle of it waiting for a fish to swim by. I'd drown before any fish would come near me. I needed a boat to fish the coral reef—or I needed to find a fishing hole in the fallen rocks somewhere near shore. I turned around and waded back to the beach where Dylan and Gerry sat watching me.

I sat down. "We need a plan," I said.

Dylan nodded. "There are conch over there." He pointed to an underwater grassy spot on the northern end of the beach. "I noticed them the first day. We motored over the spot coming in. It's not deep."

"What else?"

"The prickly pears. We've already tried them. They're all over the hill. You can eat the pear and the big leaves, the pads."

"Anything else?"

"I know a way to make water from the plants—a distillery, condensation thing."

"How do you know about that?"

"I read about it—in a book Dad had."

I squeezed his shoulder. "It's a start. We'll have conch for dinner."

The fishermen in Nassau would have been rolling on the

sand laughing if they could have seen us with the conch. It was a good thing we got an early start. It took us an hour to break into it. It took another hour to get the meat out, decide how to kill the animal—if it wasn't dead of shock already—and then cut it up. We knew we weren't going to batter it and fry it, so we cooked it like hot dogs—little pieces on the end of long sticks held over the fire. It was awful, like chewing shoe leather. And there was so little of it. One conch was barely appetizer size for the three of us. But we were worn out by the time we'd finished, and in the back of my mind was the idea that we didn't have an unlimited supply of conch. We couldn't just go out and gather them all and have a feast. We had to pace ourselves. As I lay down that night in the tent, I heard my stomach growling. The conch was a good idea, but the best we could say about it was that it would slow down starvation, not prevent it. We had to develop a bigger plan.

The next day Dylan went up on the hill to forage. It was the first time we had been apart since my solo trips to *Chrysalis* the first day. Gerry and I went together to the secret beach and searched among the tidal pools. I was hoping for crabs or lobster, but nothing showed up to let us catch it.

We went back to camp empty-handed and waited under the spinnaker for Dylan. He came back with another pear and a cactus pad. I fished out another conch, and that's all we ate that day. It was the same for two more days.

On the third day, I couldn't do anything but sleep. When I finally woke up late in the afternoon, Dylan and Gerry were busy building something with garbage bags and plastic tubes to make water, and my stomach felt like a hole gnawed through the middle of my body.

I watched them work for a while, but I was too weak to help. I escaped to the hidden beach on the other side of the rocks. Gerry's footprints were all over the sand. He must have come searching again, alone. Several tracks led to one of the half-submerged rocks. I followed them and climbed up. I lay there, sunning like an iguana and staring into the pool of water in front of me. The bottom was clear. Along the waterline of the rock were marble-size mussels of some sort. I pulled one off and tried to crack it open. Its round shape just bounced off the rock when I slammed it down.

I threw it into the middle of the pool. I'd never thought about being hungry before. Now it was all I could think about. I could see a sea urchin's black spines poking out from a crack in the bottom edge of the rock. I knew sea urchin eggs were edible. But how could you get them? All I could see was spines. I couldn't just reach in and grab.

I heard footsteps behind me and then Gerry crawled up on the rock beside me.

"Do you feel better?" he asked.

"Better?"

"You've been sleeping. You've been sick."

"I'm not sick."

"Oh." He stretched out right next to me and dropped his fingers into the water. I saw Blankie collected up under his chest. "I like it here," he said. "I like to watch the fish." He paused, but I didn't fill in the gap. "They come swimming in here and I wish I could reach down and catch them. I wish I could just grab them with my bare hands." He paused again and let both his hands play in the water. "I'm really hungry," he said, a whine edging into his voice.

I closed my eyes.

"I must be growing," he said after a while. "Whenever I was always hungry, Mom said I must be growing."

I didn't answer.

"I wish we had some milk. And cereal."

I gritted my teeth.

"Or a hot dog. Would you like a hot dog, Ben?"

I could feel my teeth grinding. I could feel my mouth watering.

"Are you hungry, too, Ben?"

"Hungry!" I exploded. I stood and felt myself towering over him. "I'm starving!" I shouted. "We're all starving."

His eyes were big now with fear, and I was afraid I would kick him. Why did he have to be so close?

I turned away and jumped off the rock into the shallow water. I splashed to the tiny beach and then tripped and fell, smacking my shin against one of the small rocks on the beach. There was a cut and it started to bleed.

I turned back to Gerry and yelled, "Now look what you did! I'm bleeding."

Then Dylan was standing close beside me, reaching out his arm. I beat it back.

"Go away," I shouted, still beating at him. "Both of you. Just leave me alone." I stumbled again and fell to the sand to sit. "I don't want—I just want—" I didn't finish.

Then Gerry was sitting on one side of me and Dylan was on the other. Dylan picked up my hand and held it, and I let him. Gerry bundled up Blankie and stuffed it in front of my face. I took it and I buried my face in it and started crying. I pressed Blankie against my eyes and my nose, and I let Dylan hold my hand, and I cried. I cried and I cried and I cried.

When I finally stopped, Dylan walked with me back to camp while Gerry stayed on the rock, hugging Blankie and peering into the pool. Dylan held me by my elbow, as if I were an old man. The air between us felt tender and broken. He told me to sit in the shade, and I sat. He brought me a cup of water, and I sipped it. He explained his evaporation and condensation apparatus for making water, and I listened.

"You're a genius," I said.

"I didn't make it up. I read about it—in a book."

"You're still a genius. You remembered it."

I wanted him to stop talking. I wanted to go back to sleep. Then Gerry's figure topped the pile of rocks and stood silhouetted against the sky. It was too much to see how skinny he looked. How long his hair had gotten. I turned away. Beside me, Dylan started laughing quietly.

"What?" Gerry asked as he got closer. There was something different in his voice.

"What have you got under your shirt?" Dylan asked.

"What do you mean?" Gerry asked.

"I mean what are you hiding under your shirt? You look pregnant."

"Don't be stupid," I said.

"Look." Dylan pulled on my arm. "Turn around and look."

I didn't have to turn. Gerry walked around and stood right in front of me.

His shirt was all pushed out over something he was hiding underneath it. He held a long stick in one hand and cupped his arms underneath the bulge in his shirt. He looked ridiculous.

"Stupid," I said. I was still quivering inside from what had happened on the secret beach, and they were acting like idiots.

"Oh!" Gerry said. "It's coming!"

Dylan had started laughing out loud and Gerry had lost his mind. "Stop it, you idiots," I said, and pushed Gerry away.

He stumbled, laughed, and lifted up his shirt. Out dropped a fish—a huge fish—a flounder at least two feet long and fifteen inches across. *Slap. Thunk.* Onto the sand. Right side up. Two eyes staring blankly at the sky. A flounder. Food. Lots of food.

Dylan whooped and jumped up and slammed Gerry in the shoulder. "A fish! Gerry, you got a fish!"

"Where did you get a fish?" I asked, just sitting there, staring at it like it was a prop that had washed up on the shore from a TV show.

"I stabbed it," Gerry said. "I stabbed it with my spear."

"Your spear?" I asked.

"Yep." He showed us his spear, a stick with a sharp point. "I lay there on the rock after you guys left and watched the water and then it came and when it was still, I put the spear in the water and waited again. And when the water was still, I shoved the spear into the fish and it died and here it is and I killed it—all by myself."

Now Dylan was hugging Gerry.

I slapped my knees. That's what I did. Just like an old man, I slapped my knees.

"You're crazy," I told Gerry. "You are a wild thing!"

Then Gerry lifted his spear into the air, yodeling like Tarzan and shouting to the sky, "Let the wild rumpus start!"

So I jumped up and I screamed and I beat on my chest and I picked up Gerry and rode him on my shoulders. Dylan marched behind us, blowing an invisible trumpet, and Gerry laughed and called orders to me in his tiny, high-pitched voice. And we all screamed and chased in circles and tore up the sand and scattered the dead leaves like confetti and ran up the hill and down again. Then Gerry stood on the rocks, waving his spear, and Dylan and I howled like dogs and then we were tired. We put our arms around each other and walked back to where the fish lay in the sand. It was our dinner and we were about to cook it, but first we stood and looked down at it and wondered at the miracle of its being there in the sand and waiting at our feet.

I squeezed Gerry's shoulder.

"Good work, buddy," I said, and he poked his tongue around in his mouth and almost smiled.

So we cooked the flounder and ate every single bite. It was huge, and we were stuffed. It was worse than Thanksgiving. I mean it was better.

I felt my stomach would explode. I felt that while I was sitting there shoving it down my throat, my arms and legs were shouting, "More! More!" And my blood was pumping it to them as fast as it could. I felt three inches taller when I stood up from that dinner. Three inches taller and about twelve inches bigger around.

Dylan didn't even bother to stand up. He just lay back flat on the sand and crossed his hands over his chest. He didn't look at the stars, either. He closed his eyes and groaned.

Gerry sat hugging Blankie, of course, and licking his fingers. One by one. Carefully. Then he gently wiped them on Blankie. Then he lifted Blankie to his face and breathed in the scent.

"You think we should have saved some?" I asked them.

"No," they both said at exactly the same time. We barely had the strength to laugh, and anyway laughing hurt too much.

"Some bunch of wild things we are," I said.

Dylan groaned again.

"I'm going to roll on over to my sand hole and curl up with my life jacket," I said.

Dylan sat slowly. "I'll waddle over with you," he said.

Gerry followed, and in the dark of the tent we slowly lowered ourselves to our beds. We were quiet, listening to the waves and the gentle breeze in the sea grape leaves. I remembered lying in bed at our old house and listening to cars on the street and trucks on the highway and even the train that went through town, blowing its whistle late at night. Now those sounds seemed like ones from a movie. Now I listened for wind and waves and sea grape leaves and the skitter of lizards outside our tent. I closed my eyes.

"I wish I had a story," Gerry said.

I started out of a half-sleep. "I'll tell you a story. Once upon a time there were three brothers shipwrecked on an island, and they were so tired, they went to sleep. Bam. End of story. Now go to sleep."

"Ben," Gerry whined.

"Shhh," Dylan said. "I'll tell you a real story. Once upon a time there was a mom named Christine."

"Dylan," I hissed.

Gerry didn't move in the dark corner where he lay.

"A mom named Christine," Dylan went on. "And she had three sons."

I could tell Gerry was breathless in the dark.

"When she nursed the littlest boy, who was a tiny baby, she held him in a white blanket. And then when he was bigger and started using a bottle, she always held the Blankie right next to his face while he drank his milk. She looked down at him and said, 'Are you my Noogie? Are you my sweetest Noogie in the world?' And he looked up at her and didn't say anything because he couldn't talk. The other two brothers wondered what a Noogie was, but they never asked. And that's the end of the story."

I realized I was as still as Gerry, that Dylan's voice had been holding me taut.

Gerry breathed loudly and slowly. "Dylan," he said accusingly, "that was a sad story."

"No, it's not. It's a happy story. It's about a mom who loved her baby very much."

"But she's gone," Gerry said in a very little voice.

"That doesn't mean she loves you any less," Dylan said.

Gerry was quiet.

And I was too. What was there to say? The present doesn't change the past. Is the fact that the past happened enough to make the present good? Is the past real? Was it still real anymore? Was Mom still alive somewhere? Was Dad?

I sat up, punched my life-jacket pillow, then lay back down. Sometimes I found it really hard to fall asleep.

CHAPTER THIRTY-FOUR

TWO DAYS LATER, Dylan caught an iguana in one of the snares he had rigged with string and boat wire. I didn't feel I had fully digested the flounder when I saw Dylan walking down the hill carrying an iguana by its tail and grinning, as if he'd just won the National Science Fair. Then he sat down to skin it and cut it up.

This was not a pretty sight. It involved a lot of blood and guts. Gerry and I tried not to watch, but there was Dylan, sitting right by the tent, smeared up to his elbows. He was totally focused, carefully ripping away the skin and setting the edible meat in a pot. When he was all done, he looked up at us and smiled.

"I hope you're hungry," he said.

We nodded, but to tell the truth, watching the whole operation had taken the edge off my appetite.

"Good," Dylan said. "Let's cook it. And we'll save the guts and stuff for fish bait. At least until they start to rot."

So that night we had roasted iguana and roasted prick-ly pears. It was actually good. We couldn't even eat it all, so Dylan wrapped it up very carefully and hung it in a tree to keep it away from crabs. In the morning, we ate the rest for breakfast. Then Gerry took Blankie and his spear and went to watch for another flounder—he could sit still all morning if he just had Blankie with him—and Dylan headed back up the hill to see what he could find.

We had been on the island about three weeks, and I was the only one who hadn't brought any food to the campfire. It was time I got off my butt and killed something for us to eat. I knew the speargun would be my weapon. But first I needed a boat to get to the outer side of the reef. That meant I had to turn the dinghy into a sailboat. And I had no idea how I was going to manage that.

Sometimes the first step toward solving the problem of building something or fixing something is to sit and look at it. You just sit and stare at it for a while and ideas float through your head and eventually one of them makes sense and sticks. This job was about how a sailboat should look. So I righted the dinghy, walked off a few steps, and then just sat and looked at it.

I thought about a lot of things besides the dinghy. I thought about the girl who used to come ride in my imaginary car. I thought about Mom. I thought about the southeastern shore of this island and how it was a straight drop into the sea. I thought about what Dad's hands looked like on the tiller and how his eyes squinted when he looked up to check the set of the sails.

And I remembered one time on the lake when we were in the rowboat and I had lost one of the oars overboard. Dad stood up in the middle of the boat, unbuttoned his shirt, and held it open wide. Then he turned himself until he was set the way a sail would have been. "Use that oar for a rudder," he said. I stuck the oar in the water at the stern of the boat to steer and watched us begin to inch through the water as the wind caught Dad's shirt. We had sailed with no mast, no sail, no tiller, and no rudder. If Dad could turn a rowboat into a sailboat that easily, then surely I could manage.

It came to me in lurches. The spinnaker pole for a mast. Cut a piece out of the jib for a sail. We had plenty of lines. With the toolbox I ought to be able to use some branches to make an all-in-one tiller and rudder. That center ridge of a palm frond had a nice flat surface that would work well. A boom? We didn't need a boom. This wasn't going to be a fancy sailboat. It was just going to take me to the reef and back.

I walked to the tent and yanked out the spinnaker pole. The tent collapsed, but I had begun the boat. Five days later, the tent was fixed and the sailboat was finished.

When Dylan and Gerry came to admire it, I showed them how I had lashed the spinnaker pole to the forward seat through a new hole, how I had stabilized the top with makeshift shrouds, and how I had used the old head and grommet on the tack to attach my handkerchief sail to the mast. Even the tiller-rudder was complete—two palm-frond spines bolted together at an angle.

It wasn't pretty, but it sailed. Of course, it couldn't point. The closest I could sail to the wind was about sixty degrees. Still, if I had to tack and was willing to go slow, I could get where I wanted to go.

"You're a genius," Dylan said, admiring my handiwork, but Gerry's mind was on something different. He stayed behind even after Dylan had gone back to stalking iguanas. He went with me on a short sail to the reef and back. He helped me tidy up afterward.

When we were walking back to camp, he reached out and took my hand. "Ben." He tugged slightly, and I looked down at him. "Now we can go find Dad," he said.

I stopped still. It's not very often that a door opens and all of a sudden you see life from another person's completely different point of view. But here was Gerry's shining face and all his happiness laid out for me like that, and suddenly I understood. All the time between waking up and finding Dad gone and this day when the dinghy became a sailboat was an interlude of unreality for Gerry.

"What do you mean, Gerry?"

"We can go back now to where we were when the storm hit us, and then we can find Dad."

It was so simple to him. Rewind the tape. Rewrite the show. Do a better job with the end this time.

I wished Dylan were with us. I knew the words I wanted to say were cruel. I closed my eyes against the brightness of the sun. I felt the hardness of Gerry's slender fingers in my palm.

"And then," he said, "we can go back home—all of us together."

"Gerry—" I started. But what could I say? Anything I said would hurt, because the truth was cruel. So I cheated—I lied. "A fishing boat has already found Dad by now. Now he is looking for us. The best thing for us to do is to wait here. If we stay in one place, it will be easier for him to find us."

"Someone is coming to get us?"

I looked in his eyes. Blue. Sky blue. You've heard that phrase all your life and then you look in someone's eyes and there it is—sky blue eyes. It's a shock. Especially if you're looking into eyes you've seen almost every day of your life for six years.

"Yes," I said.

He looked back at me. "Good," he said quietly. He sighed a little. "I hope they come soon."

CHAPTER THIRTY-FIVE

EVERY MORNING AFTER that, I took the dinghy-sailboat to the reef and tried to spear fish. I had thought it would be easy, but it was not. I ended up spearing a lot of coral. I managed to nab a reef lobster a few times so I wouldn't come back empty-handed. I figured out how to roll the sea urchins over and out of their hiding places and how to pick them up with sticks. We learned to eat them too. But the only fish I got was the one I found trapped in a ball of sargassum that tangled on my anchor line.

And the dinghy was not as good a sailboat as I had hoped. I spent a lot of time repairing it or, if the wind was in the wrong direction, sailing forever to get to a spot a hundred yards away. It was a frustrating business.

Still, it was a peaceful, mystical world on the reef. It was different from all the other reefs we had seen because I knew this one. I swam it every day. I was not surprised to see the huge brain coral because I had seen it before. I would have been surprised if it had been gone. And the staghorns and sea feathers were where they were supposed to be. They waved there just as they had done the day before, their colors changing with the slant of the sun, their direction shifting with the current but always exactly in the same place every day. I came to recognize the flash of shadow that was an octopus suddenly sucking himself into his hiding place. I saw the tiny garden eels that lived in the sand with just their heads poking out until I rippled the water too close. I saw the brilliant blue Pederson shrimp that groomed the coral, eating away the slime or mold that would have made the coral sick. I almost felt I recognized the school of neon gobies that flashed in unison across the maze on the face of the brain coral.

But even though I got to know the reef, I never saw any fish big enough to spear. Maybe it was the tides. Maybe I was too noisy. I decided to try chumming, baiting the area with pieces of leftover fish or meat. The chum attracts the fish, and then you get a good shot. The very first time I did it, the chum worked. A big grouper came by to investigate but I wasn't ready. My shot missed. By the time I'd reeled in my line and cocked the gun again, the grouper and the chum were gone. Another day empty-handed. I tried again the next day and missed again. I decided I needed to hunt where my dwindling supply of chum would attract more than one grouper. I decided to fish near the rocks that fell off the secret beach and rolled like giant stepping-stones into the ocean.

Here the reef began to break apart so that dark blue fingers of ocean reached up to the fallen rocks and made deep protected pools. I was hoping that the deeper water right next to the half-submerged rock had created a feeding ground the fish couldn't pass up. It would be harder to fish here because of the danger of the rocks and the difficulty anchoring. But I decided to try.

The day was almost windless and the seas were calm when I anchored the dinghy at the end of the string of rocks, snagging the flukes in a shallow, sandy drift between two rocks. From my anchorage at the rock farthest away from the island, I could see Gerry clearly where he lay on his flat rock, Blankie tucked under his chin, his spear tip quiet in the water. Dylan was climbing the side of the island, carrying an old shirt to bring home whatever he found that we could use. He waved to me when he saw me round the rocks, and Gerry looked up when he heard the splash of my anchor.

The waves broke gently against the rock where Gerry lay, but out where I was they just sloshed weakly against the rounded rocks and then fell quietly away. I rocked in the dinghy a moment, feeling the sun hot on my head. Then I picked up the chum wrapped in a scrap of old sail and the speargun and slipped silently into the water.

Here the water was cooler and darker, but I could still see. From underwater, I could tell that these were not rocks that had rolled off the mountain and landed in the ocean. Instead, they were like the chunks of ice that break off an iceberg, huge sections of the island that had broken away and sunk slowly sideways into the ocean, so that only the tops were now left above water. Their steep underwater sides were crusted with sharp coral and teeming with tiny fish. Sea urchin spines rose like black spears out of the crevices. Right next to my left elbow an anemone waved the purple tips of its light green tentacles. The water was so rich, I could feel the fish around me just waiting to be caught.

I swam in a tight circle, dropping the chum in three different spots, then surfaced for breath. In the bright sun, I could see Dylan a little higher up the side of the hill. Again he was turned to me. Again he was waving. I took in a deep breath and dove.

The water filled my ears. The tiny fish swam within inches of my gun. Then suddenly there were three grouper gliding toward the chum. The sun was overhead, but my shadow was safely behind me. I was slightly above the largest fish, looking at his side. I aimed. I led him slightly. I pulled the trigger. *Ping. Swish. Thunk.* In an instant two of the grouper disappeared. But the third, the largest, was still there, suspended in the water with my dart piercing it just over its gills. I had made the perfect shot. The fish was paralyzed in the water. I had done it. Finally, I had speared a fish. I turned to take my prize home.

Thirty feet away and cruising slowly closer was a giant hammerhead shark. Gray, long, and relentless, he swung his flat, evil face gently from side to side as he pinpointed me in the water where I was floating in the center of a circle of chum and holding a large, bleeding fish.

I couldn't move. I just stared at him. He was twice as big as I was, and he took up the whole ocean between the dinghy and me. I needed to surface to breathe or to swim away or to climb the coral-crusted side of the rock. But I could not move.

I heard my own blood rushing in my ears and believed I felt the push of the water from the lumbering movement of his head. He swam toward me deliberately and slowly. There was no need for him to hurry. There was nothing I could do.

Then the water exploded beside me into a tornado of bubbles and noise. I saw boy legs treading water furiously and kicking in the clear blue. And there were boy hands slapping the surface of the water and sending harsh sounds ricocheting into the currents. The hypnotic spell broke and I pushed myself to the surface gasping for air. Gerry and Dylan were swimming beside me, kicking and yelling and slapping the water. The shark's fin stopped. He was frozen in the water and facing the three of us.

"Throw him the fish, you idiot!" Dylan yelled.

I ripped the shaft out of the grouper and threw the fish hard and far out into the water.

The fin paused, then turned slowly and sliced toward the exact spot in the ocean where the grouper was now sinking.

Then the shark was gone too, and the three of us were swimming there in the water, hearts pounding and breath ragged.

"You idiots!" I screamed at them. "You could have—"

"Noise," Dylan panted. "Scares them."

We were gasping and slowly treading water when we both suddenly looked at Gerry.

He was pumping his arms and legs desperately. He blew out his breath in puffs as he barely kept his head above the water. My arm flashed out and grabbed him.

"Let go," he said quickly. His eyes darted to the boat and I let go.

"Can you make it all the way to the dinghy?" I asked.

He looked at the side of the rock he had just jumped from. It was too steep and high to climb. His arms and legs worked frantically. Then he nodded quickly and began to dig his way slowly through the ocean, spitting water and blinking hard.

"Hold your fingers together like a cup," Dylan said. "That helps."

Gerry instantly tightened his fingers together.

"Try to keep your butt a little higher," I said. "It makes your legs work better for you."

We could see him trying. Dylan and I slowly cruised beside him. It was so easy for us. It was so hard for him. His eyes never turned from the dinghy. He did not look to us for help. He kicked and spat and splashed and blinked. And he made it to the dinghy all alone. Dylan climbed in first and grabbed him under his arms. I shoved him under his butt, and we threw him in.

"When did you learn to swim?" I asked Gerry.

He shrugged and looked away. He was shaking.

I unfurled our makeshift sail and pointed us toward our beach. There wasn't really enough room in the dinghy for all of us, now that I had rigged the sail through the forward seat, but the wind was with us and we were only ten minutes from shore. Gerry sat slumped and gasping for air until we landed and hauled the dinghy up the beach. Once again I had no fish.

"Thanks," I said to them both.

"Sure," Dylan said, already heading back to camp.

I stooped and looked Gerry in the face. "That was brave," I said.

He dipped his head in a silent nod.

"Why did you do it?"

"Because you're my brother," he said, and waited quietly to help me furl the sail.

CHAPTER THIRTY-SIX

THAT NIGHT THERE were so many stars that even Dylan couldn't talk about them. With no moon, they were like glitter spilled across the sky, all merging into one another in their brilliance. We just lay on our backs on the beach and looked up and were silent.

"Aren't you going to tell a star story?" Gerry finally asked Dylan.

"No," Dylan said. "Not tonight."

"I need a story," Gerry said.

Dylan was quiet for a few seconds then answered, "I'll tell a Baby Gerry story."

"Okay." Gerry wiggled a little to settle himself better in the sand.

"Once upon a time there was a mom named Christine and she had two sons."

"What about me?" Gerry asked.

"This is about when you got born."

"Oh."

"She told her two sons, 'Boys, you are going to have a baby brother or sister.' Then one day, she made a funny sound and Dad rushed her to the hospital and when you were a boy, she said, 'Perfect.'"

"You're making that part up," I said. "You don't know what she said."

"That's okay," Gerry said. "I don't mind."

"Anyway," Dylan continued, "that night Dad took us to see you and I gave you one of my army men. I wanted to name you Timmy."

"But they named me Gerry."

"Actually," I said, "they named you Gerard, but every time we tried to say it we choked. So you got to be Gerry."

"I like Gerry."

"It fits you," Dylan said. "Anyway, when I came home from nursery school the next day, Mom and you were back from the hospital and she let me hold you. You were all wrapped up in Blankie, and you were wiggly, like a puppy. When she took you back, you threw up on your clothes, so she told me to go upstairs and get you something clean to wear. I didn't know where your things were, so I brought my Batman pajama shirt. It's a good thing it was my short-sleeved one. The end."

"That story is more about you than me."

"Well, it's what I remember."

"I want a story about me."

Then a memory shot into my head. "I have a story about you, Gerry. Just you. Dylan, remember that time when Gerry was really little and Dad came home from work just as Mom was finishing giving him his bottle? And Dad was sitting there, reading the paper, but she wanted him to hold Gerry while she cooked dinner? So she was kind of pretending that Gerry was jumping up over the paper? And Dad put the paper down and looked up at Gerry with this big, goofy, openmouthed look, like goo-goo, gaa-gaa or something, and Gerry just kind of looks down at him and—*blugh*—throws up right into Dad's mouth!"

Dylan howled. "I remember! I remember! And remember Mom just stands there and says, 'Oh. I forgot to burp him.'"

"You guys!" Gerry said. He was trying to act upset but he was laughing too. A little, anyway. "Stop it," he said. But we couldn't stop laughing.

I sat up. "Oh, I forgot to burp him," I said, and let go the biggest burp I could. It was a good one. Dylan's was better, though. "My Noogie," I said, and grabbed Gerry and rubbed his head with my knuckles.

"Stop!" Gerry said. "Just stop." He pushed my hand away and then shoved at my chest. "It's not fair."

"Not fair?" asked Dylan.

"I'm stupid in all those stories."

"No. You're a baby," Dylan said. "Babies do stuff like that. They're *babies*."

"Wait," I said. "Don't feel bad, Gerry. I'll tell one on Dylan. This is when he was about two, so I was about seven. He was just starting to talk, and he played this game called 'What's in there?' He would go around and point at cabinets and boxes and pots and say 'What's in there?' and Mom, of course, would always show him. So one night Mom and Dad are having this party for only grown-ups, but Dylan and I are hanging around with them until bedtime. And all of them are standing in the kitchen drinking beer and Dylan cruises in and looks up at Dad leaning back against the counter. And then Dylan points right at Dad's fly and says, 'What's in there?'"

"Did not!" Dylan shouted.

"Did too," I said. "I remember because this one guy standing right beside Dad had a mouthful of beer and he spewed it out all over me. And they all started laughing and slapping the countertop and Mom was wiping me off with a kitchen towel and Dylan was standing there staring and Dad scooped him up and said, 'That's my boy,' and—"

And then I remembered that Dad had had on jeans. I remembered hugging up next to his leg. I remembered his hand in my hair. I remembered he had reached down and rubbed me between my shoulder blades and then his hand came up and curved over my shoulder and squeezed and he looked down at me and smiled and said, "Bedtime."

"And what else?" Gerry asked.

"And it's the truth. The whole story is the complete, absolute truth. I didn't make up one word."

We lay back down again and laughed a little more and watched the stars.

Then out of the night came Gerry's voice. "Was Mom as pretty as I remember?"

"Yes," I said.

"Did she smell good?"

"Always."

"Did she really give me Blankie, Dylan?"

"God's truth," said Dylan.

"I miss her," Gerry said, but Dylan and I said nothing.

CHAPTER THIRTY-SEVEN

SO WE SETTLED into living on the island. We carefully rationed our water from *Chrysalis*, but we also knew how to find water in secret places in the rocks and the palm-frond crotches. Dylan's three water stills each made about a cup a day and sometimes more. Gerry got good at fishing with a line and hook as well as with his spear. Dylan could catch an iguana and even brought home several birds. He was always harvesting something from the hill. First it was the cactus and then some kind of plum from a bush with fierce thorns. I, of course, fished the reef. One night we watched from under the spinnaker as a turtle made her way up the beach, dug a hole with her flippers, and laid her eggs. We agreed to let the turtle go, but we did eat the eggs.

We weren't hungry anymore. We weren't thirsty. We knew

how to live on the island. It had taken a long time, but we had figured it out.

Then the day came when it all started to unravel. When that day dawned, we did what we always did. Dylan set off up the hill to explore and forage. Gerry took Blankie to the secret beach to build pebble forts, watch crabs, and maybe catch something. I went to the reef to fish, now always mindful of the sharks.

I came back a little later than usual with three good-size grouper. Gerry was already back at camp, but he was empty-handed today. He sampled a sea grape while I cleaned the fish, cutting two of them into paper-thin strips to hang on a branch to dry. Gerry spit out the grape. "Yetch. Sour."

"Dylan said it would be a while."

"He's right."

"Gerry, do you remember how Mom used to do that fish thing where she wrapped it in paper to cook it?"

He shook his head.

"Oh, well." I cleaned the third fish and decided that maybe I'd try wrapping it in sea grape leaves. I'd ask Dylan what he thought when he got back.

But he didn't come back. We waited and waited. After it was dark, I realized we'd waited too long. Dylan wouldn't come back in the dark. There were too many places he could fall. He was out on the hill somewhere now, sitting out the night. But why hadn't he come back while it was still light?

"When is Dylan coming?" Gerry asked.

"After a while," I said.

"I'm hungry. Can we go ahead and eat?"

I forgot about the sea grape leaves and cooked the fish quickly in the frying pan with a little water. Of course, by now we didn't really care whether or not it was cooked. We could eat it raw and still enjoy it. That night we chewed our fish silently and then cleaned up. I banked the fire and sent Gerry to bed. "I'll wait up for Dylan," I said.

I didn't sleep that night. As tired as I was with fishing and swimming, I thought I would surely doze. But every breeze, every clack of leaves, every slither of a lizard or patter of a crab was Dylan coming home. I kept planning what I would say. "How dare you stay out late. Gerry's been so worried. I finally sent him to bed. You can apologize in the morning." Then the hours passed, and it was, "We've been worried sick. Don't ever do that again." And later "Thank God you're back. Are you okay?" Then the sun started to come up and the world turned the flat, charcoal gray of a cloudy sunrise.

It's surprising how long it takes the sun to come up all the way when you're waiting. Complete sunrise took about two hours, I guess, from the time I noticed the sky starting to get light until the time I figured it was light enough for me to go wake Gerry and break the news. He understood at once.

"You stay here," I told him, "in case he comes back into camp. I'll go look."

Gerry nodded.

"Don't even go over to the secret beach. Just stay here."

He nodded again.

"And if he comes back, make a lot of noise. Bang the hammer on something or whatever. You figure it out. I may hear you. I may not. But try."

"Okay," he said.

I tied the jar of water and a knife into my shirt and put on my shoes. "Good luck," Gerry said. I lifted my hand in good-bye and headed up the hill.

I hadn't thought until that long, long night about how big our island was. I was standing there just beyond the band of trees and looking up the hill, thinking that searching by myself was going to be like trying to color in a whole piece of paper with a ballpoint pen. It would take me hours to cover the whole island. Did the hours matter? Was there a quicker way? I had no choice, and the only way to start was to start. So I did, plotting a low, zigzag trail that would carry me back and forth across the face of the hill, slowly climbing, slowly searching.

Of course, I called his name as I walked. I called his name and I looked all around me, 360 degrees. Up and down. At big bushes I stopped and looked underneath. All over the hill were signs that he had been there. I found his snares. I found two traps. I saw where he had cut the leaves from the prickly pears. I saw scrabblings in the dirt that must have been a chase. Maybe after the birds. The hillside had changed since we first hiked it. Now it was Dylan's. I saw signs of him everywhere, but I didn't see him.

Then I remembered the cliffs on the southeastern side.

The cliffs that dropped straight into the water. "Oh, my God," I said out loud. I stopped in my tracks and looked up to where the island's summit met the sky and I knew. I knew exactly where Dylan was, and my throat closed in while my feet started pounding straight up the hill.

My brain was in overdrive. Ledges. Were there ledges? I could swear I remembered ledges. How far down? How wide? How many? Why would any fool go close to the edge? Dylan was too smart to do that. I was panicking. I was crazy. He would never—Oh God, I'm sure he did. That's where he is. Please let him be okay. Please let him not be hurt. Please let him—And my mind froze at the image of him plummeting straight down into the water, the waves picking up his body and throwing him back against the rocks. Once. Twice. Stop! Stop! A rope. I should have brought a rope. But I never imagined. Never. Never.

And then I stood on the edge of the cliffs, and I was dizzy. I fell to my hands and knees and called, but the wind swept my voice away. A little closer to the edge and I looked down. Straight down. No ledges. Straight into the waves below. I felt my stomach clutch, and I rolled over on my back and closed my eyes.

"Steady," I told myself. "Steady."

I rolled back over and forced myself to look right and left along the cliffs. And then I saw his shirttail fluttering in the breeze. He was lying on a wide ledge about thirty feet to my left and ten feet down. Above him was another small ledge about two feet down. On that ledge was a hawk's nest. Suddenly I understood. He had been looking for eggs and he fell. He had crawled up against the cliff face—in fear or cold—and lay there, curled into a knot with only his shirttail flapping in the wind.

I stood. "Steady," I said. "We can do this." I walked toward him and lay down again. When I looked over the edge, I could see his face. His eyes were open. He was blinking and staring at the rock. "Dylan," I called, and he looked up.

"I knew you'd come," he said.

"I'll have to go back and get a rope," I said. "Then I can help you climb back."

"I can't climb," he said. "My leg."

Only then did I notice—the sickening bend in his leg halfway between knee and ankle and the terrifying sliver of white bone breaking through the skin and surrounded by torn flesh and dried blood.

"My God," I said.

"I broke it," he said. "It hurts." His voice choked and he sucked in air suddenly.

"Steady," I told him. "We'll get you. Be calm. I've got to go back for supplies."

He nodded.

"I'll be back soon. I mean, as soon as I can."

He nodded again.

"You'll be okay? I mean—"

He nodded again. "Go," he said.

So I did, flying and jumping and crashing and sometimes even rolling down the hill. At camp I gathered lines and Gerry. "Bring your spear," I told him. "And Blankie."

When we got back, Dylan was still staring at the rock, and the sun was a lot higher and hotter. I tied Blankie and the spear together in a tight package with the smallest line. "When I ask for them," I said to Gerry, "let them over the edge."

"You're going over?" Gerry asked.

"Somebody has to go."

Little stubby, dwarf trees grew near the cliff edge, but they were all we had. I grabbed one and pulled as hard as I could. It came up, roots and all, and I fell over backwards. I stood up, threw it away, and tried another. That one held. I was praying for a taproot that went all the way to China while I tied the line into a saddle around my thighs and waist. I wound the rope twice around the tree and held the loose end. I'd never done any rock climbing, but I'd seen it on TV. And we'd had to climb the rope in gym. My arms were strong, I knew. I looked over my shoulder at the empty space behind me.

You have to, I told myself. *It's all up to you.*

"Steady. Steady. Steady," I whispered over and over as I inched over the edge of the island and bumped my way down to where Dylan lay.

"Okay, Gerry," I said. "Send them down." I couldn't look up. It would have been too scary. But I knew Gerry's eyes were showing just over the edge, watching us.

"Dylan," I said. "I'm going to hurt you."

"I know," he said. "Is it okay if I cry?"

"Fine by me," I said.

One thing I will never be is a doctor. I felt dizzier than ever looking at the sharp white point of Dylan's bone and the gash in his skin. The blood was dark and dried up all over his leg and on the ledge too. His hands were bloody where he had felt his wound. There was blood on his face and in his hair where his wet, bloody hands had touched.

"Okay," I said to myself. "Okay. Let's go. Let's do this thing." And I reached out and scooped up Dylan just enough to turn him over on his back so I could straighten out his knee. Tears were pouring out from under his closed eyelids and his lips were quivering. "Cry," I said. "Cry out loud."

Then I lifted the broken leg and Dylan groaned. The bone moved and new blood came out. "Please. Oh, please," I said. "Oh, God." I wrapped his leg in Blankie, pulling the thin worn fabric as tight as I could. Then I tied the spear alongside the broken bone and then up above his knee, too, so even that joint couldn't move. I tied the lines tight, trying to cut off the blood supply because I knew the worst was still to come.

Dylan's face was white and he was staring at the rock. "You can't faint yet, Dylan," I said.

He nodded.

"We've got to get you back up."

He nodded again.

So then I started tying a saddle on him. "Can you hold on?" I asked.

He nodded again, but this time I didn't believe him. I took the line off his thighs and started tying him around his chest and under his arms. "We're going to drag you up," I said. "I'm going back up now. You'll feel us pulling soon."

I don't remember pulling myself back over the edge of the cliff. It must not have been hard. Gerry was waiting there for me, and I handed him the end of the rope that was now tied around Dylan. He wrapped it around the same tree. Then we walked to the edge of the cliff and began to pull. Instantly we felt Dylan's weight and heard him groan.

I was praying Dad had taught me right about knots. I was praying the tree held. I was praying Dylan didn't bleed to death before we got him up. We dragged him to the edge and saw his hands grabbing at the grass. We pulled him a little farther and there was the top of his head and then his face and his arms stretched out across the dirt and then finally his chest was up and he was lying hanging halfway over still and I grabbed him under his arms and pulled him completely to safety and then he fainted.

I carried Dylan back to camp. Gerry walked beside me, carrying the ropes. His face was white, but he kept going. Dylan stayed out the whole way down and it was just as well because it was a pretty rough ride. I laid him flat on the beach and built up the fire and got all our clean water and started it boiling. Then I unwrapped him and cleaned him up as best I could and looked at the bone, trying to decide what to do.

Or I should say trying to decide if I really had to do what

I thought I had to do. From somewhere back in some TV-Western memory I thought that what I had to do was to pull on his leg really hard so that the bone would slide back into place. I couldn't do that. It would hurt him too much.

I looked at his face and he was watching me. "You have to jerk it," he said. "You have to grab my foot and jerk really hard."

"You're kidding," I said.

"No. In fact, you probably ought to tie me up to a tree or something and then jerk or else I'll just go dragging through the sand and it won't work."

"Dylan, I can't hurt you like that."

"I'll try to pass out again if that will make it easier."

So I did what he said. I sat him up next to a tree and tied him at the hips as tight as I could. I had to tie him at the chest, too, though, because fortunately he did pass out again—and without trying. Gerry wanted to help, but it was too much for him. All he could do was cry. I finally told him to go in the tent and leave me alone.

When I had Dylan tied as tight as I could get him, I lifted up his foot. I knew it wouldn't do any good to pull gently and slowly. The pain would kill him. The only way to do it was to pull suddenly and hard. I felt myself sweating. I felt his round heel in my hand. His face was streaked with blood and dirt and sweat and tears. His hands were limp in the sand. And there was this bone still staring at me.

"Now!" I shouted, and pulled with all the strength I had

left in my body, and the bone slid down into the gash and disappeared.

And Dylan screamed. The pain brought him to and he screamed.

And it started bleeding again. Oh God, how much blood could he lose?

I pushed Blankie against the wound and Dylan screamed again. I washed him and started jabbering. I don't know what I was saying. I took long sticks and tied them to either side of his leg. I talked and talked and talked. But Dylan didn't hear a word because he was out again.

Thank God.

Then I was done. The bone was inside, the wound was clean, and the straight sticks were tied to hold it secure.

Now all Dylan had to do was heal. It would take time, but that was one thing we had plenty of.

CHAPTER THIRTY-EIGHT

EXCEPT DYLAN DIDN'T heal. We didn't know it at first. At first he did a lot of sleeping. For about a day, he would rouse up for just a minute and we'd drip a little water into him and maybe squeeze a little prickly pear pulp between his teeth. He'd get the stuff down and look around and smile like a goofball. Then he'd turn his head sideways and go back to sleep. I figured his body knew what was best, and if I'd been camping on an exposed rock ledge for almost twenty-four hours with a compound fracture bleeding all over the place—well, I figured I would want to sleep too.

Then he was awake. He was feeling so much better, he told us. Gerry became Mr. Entertainment for him and brought him shells to admire or plants to identify. Gerry took over the water-making thing and brought the water to Dylan every day.

I fished harder than ever and caught plenty. I wished we had milk—milk for strong bones. Dylan said he would eat the fish bones if I would quit talking about milk.

After a few days, Dylan said he felt good enough for me to carry him down to the water. He said he needed to soak his leg. He thought that would be good for it. So I picked him up and set him back down very gently in the edge. It must have hurt. His face was white again. He said he felt fine. So I started taking him down every day. We fixed up a place where he could lean back against a rock and let his leg rest in the water. We even made him a little shade with palm fronds.

His wound looked good. It was red, of course, and it would have looked a whole lot better if somebody could have stitched it. But it wasn't all horrible and swollen. It wasn't oozing pus. I felt good being the nurse. I felt we had the routine down. I knew what to do every day. Breakfast. Boil water. Clean wound. Feed Dylan. Set him in the water. Go fish. At night, build fire. Cook fish. Lie on beach. Tell stories. I could do this. Dylan seemed better every day. We were going to get past even this.

But something changed. I couldn't tell what it was at first. It just seemed as if the color of the air had shifted somehow. Then I realized that Dylan had stopped smiling. His mouth was set in a straight line, and when he thought we weren't looking at him, his eyes were vague and worried. I realized he was hurting, not just when I moved him, but all the time.

So when Gerry was off hunting up some shells to show Dylan, I sat down beside him instead of heading for the reef.

"What's up?" I asked.

"Nothing."

"I mean, what's wrong?"

"My leg is broken."

"Yeah, I noticed." I looked him straight in the eye, and he looked away. I took his chin in my hand and turned it back to me. "Seriously, Dylan. Something new is wrong. What is it?"

Tears stood suddenly along the bottom curve of his eyes. A finger of ice pierced me.

He took in a deep breath and let it go quickly. Then again. I knew it was a way to keep his voice level when he talked.

"I think, Ben, that something inside is infected. It hurts in a different way. And now, when I touch it with my fingertips, just the touching hurts."

"Infected?"

He nodded.

"But there's no pus. It's not all red. We've kept it clean."

"I know."

"It can't be."

"Touch here, Ben. Gently. With the flat of your hand."

I did. "It's hot."

He nodded. "That's infection."

"Bodies get over infection all the time," I said. "That's what white blood cells are for."

"Yeah," he said. "It's just that it hurts."

I nodded. I patted his shoulder. "Don't worry. We'll take care of you." And then I left to swim the reef.

Dylan didn't eat as well that night. I was fussing at Gerry about wasting food when I noticed Dylan hadn't eaten his. "What's the matter? You're not hungry?" He barely shook his head. "It's okay," I said. "You need more rest."

In the tent that night, I could hear Dylan twisting and occasionally sniffing. I felt fear again. What do you do without medicine? When just cleaning it isn't enough? Was there a plant we didn't know about? Some tree bark? A special seaweed? I would dive for it. All the way down. I would push away the fire coral to reach it. I would rip it out from under a starving shark. *Whatever it takes,* I said to myself. *Whatever it takes.* Then I waited through a long night and a silent breakfast and a flat good-bye to Gerry as he headed for his beach before I went to ask Dylan what it would take to make him well.

He was lying still in the tent, his hands resting on his chest, his eyes looking up. The tent smelled bad and I thought I ought to clean it.

"Hey, Dylan."

He shifted slightly.

"You're not better."

He shook his head.

"You need to get your white blood cells busy, man."

He didn't smile.

I picked up a little stick and snapped it in two. "You're even worse, aren't you."

"Yes."

"How?" I asked.

"Touch me," he said.

I touched his arm. It was too warm. "You have fever," I said.

"Look at my leg—under the sticks."

I looked. The sticks had been disguising it, but now it was clear. An ugly blotch of red discolored his calf. His ankle was swollen. The delicate edges of his kneecap were disappearing into the swelling at his knee.

I looked away.

"Do you know of something?" I asked. "Some plant? A weird cactus, a seaweed?"

He was quiet.

"Do you, Dylan? I'll go get it. Whatever it is. I can—"

"I don't know of anything."

"Some book you've read—something of Dad's. Surely they said something."

"I don't know of anything."

"Think harder, Dylan."

"Ben. What do you think I've been doing lying here all this time?"

I paused. "You mean there's nothing?"

"There's nothing. That I know of. That will help."

"So?"

"So my body either gets better by itself—or I die."

That was a word that sucked all the other words out of me. There were no soft edges to it. There was no way to pretend it meant something else. I had to let the reverberations slowly ring out of my head before I could think again.

"We'll take you to a doctor," I said.

Dylan sniffed. "Yeah, right. Why don't you call for an appointment."

"I'm serious, Dylan. I'll take you to a doctor. Whatever it takes, I'll do it."

"What doctor? Where? In what vehicle?" Now he was tired.

"I don't know. We'll go in the dinghy. Surely there's another island nearby. We've just never tried."

Dylan was looking away now. "Yes. I think you're right about another island. Probably not all that far in a real boat. But in the dinghy? Never. And we don't even know what direction to go in."

"West. We'd go west. I've seen clouds—cumulus—low on the horizon. They say that's a sign of an island."

"Ben. We don't know how far. And we can't all fit in the dinghy."

"We can do it. If we try hard enough, I'm sure—"

"Ben. Go away. I'm tired." He turned his head and covered his face with his arm.

I crawled outside the tent and turned to head for the dinghy. And there was Gerry, sitting just on the other side of the tent canvas from where Dylan lay. He didn't look at me. He stabbed a stick in the sand over and over. Blankie lay on the ground beside him. I took his arm gently and pulled him to stand. I handed him Blankie and led him away down the beach. I sat with my back propped against the dinghy and pulled Gerry into my lap. He was stiff at first, then he slowly relaxed. He put his head against my chest. I wrapped him with my arms and pulled him close. He was small and sandy. He was trembling. We listened to the water slap. A few pelicans floated on a quiet corner of our bay. The terns plunged for the kill and the seagulls called out their single word, "Die! Die! Die!"

By afternoon, Dylan was clearly worse. Mom used to say she knew we were sick by our eyes. Dylan's eyes looked worse than sick. Sometimes, it seemed he was looking somewhere else—as if there were a play going on in front of him that we couldn't see. Sometimes his face was too pink and sometimes it had no color at all. He was restless and breathing too fast. But he was talking clearly. And giving us instructions.

"Be sure not to cut too much of one prickly pear at a time," he said to me.

"What are you talking about?"

"You don't want to kill the plant. Think of it like pruning."

"Right, Dylan."

"Gerry knows how to work the water-maker. The theory is condensation. You put the plants in the bottom of the pit and the water evaporates out of them and condenses on the garbage bag stretched over it. Then the condensation drips into the cup."

"Right, Dylan."

"Did you know Gerry has a loose tooth?"

"What?"

"Take care of it when it comes out. It will be useful some way."

I couldn't take it anymore. "Let's go, Gerry," I said. "Let's put him in the dinghy. We're going to a doctor."

"No!" Dylan shouted. "Don't move me. It would hurt! In a dinghy, on the waves. No. I'm sorry. I couldn't."

"You're jabbering, Dylan," I said. "You'll do fine."

"We can't all fit in the dinghy, Ben," Gerry said quietly. "With the sail, there isn't enough room."

"He needs a doctor," I said.

"Then you go get one," Gerry said, and pulled Blankie slowly over his head.

That evening when I touched Dylan's forehead, it was blazing hot. He was moaning slightly. I filled a pot with seawater and bathed Dylan's face and hands. I lifted his shirt and bathed his chest. "Don't," he said. "That hurts."

"We need to get your fever down."

He twisted away from the cloth when I touched his face.

"Come on, Dylan," I begged. "You've got to get better."

"Leave me alone," he muttered.

So I lifted him and took him down to the edge of the water. The moon was clear tonight—not a full moon, but a lovely rocking crescent sitting above the eastern rise of our island. It reflected in long, liquid squiggles on the ripples in the water's edge. I waded with Dylan into the water and then sat down, holding him in my arms.

"Once upon a time," I said, "there was a guy who had two little brothers. And when one of them was sick, this guy wanted to make him well, but he didn't know how."

Dylan's eyes were open in the darkness. I could see the shimmer of moon reflecting in them. He was not looking at me.

"This guy said he would do anything—whatever it took—to make his brother well. But it seemed there was nothing he could do. Until one day, the littlest brother said, 'You go,' and then the guy knew that the only thing he could do was the hardest thing of all."

Dylan's gaze had shifted and now he was looking at me.

"Because to go alone meant to leave both of them—the one who was hurt and the one who was too little to take care of himself. If the biggest brother could get help, they would all be okay in the end. But if he was gone too long or if he was lost at sea, then both the little brothers—alone on the island—who could tell?"

Dylan closed his eyes. I brushed some water on his forehead. It seemed cooler. Some drops rolled over his face, and I smoothed them off his eyes. He opened his eyes again, blinking. "Don't go," he said. "Don't leave Gerry alone."

"We'll ask him," I said. "We'll leave it up to him."

I carried Dylan carefully back to the tent and laid him down. The heat radiated off of him like a banked fire. The stench was strong in the tent and I realized at last that it was Dylan's leg. I took Gerry outside and asked him what I should do. He didn't answer right away. He held Blankie over his mouth and looked out at the dark ocean and then at the dinghy.

"You would come right back?" he asked.

"As soon as I could—if I could."

"You're a good sailor," he said.

"I try."

"You wouldn't fall off the boat?"

"No. I wouldn't do that."

He clutched Blankie tighter. "Do you want me to help you pack?"

I took one jar of water, a few strips of dried fish, some prickly-pear pads already scraped clean, and a hook and line. It all fit easily into an old shirt tied up in a knot. I threw an extra line in the bottom of the dinghy for good measure. It seemed a sailorly thing to do. The boat would be ready to leave when morning came again.

Dylan lay in the soft bed we had scooped out for him. Gerry stood on the beach, dragging a stick around in the sand. I stood by Dylan, watching the moon set. The crescent lay on its back, open to the stars above it. It sank slowly down behind our little island until all I could see were the two tips of the crescent, almost like horns standing above the tops of the trees. Then one horn disappeared behind a higher rock. Then the second horn went and the sky was dark. I heard Gerry dragging the stick behind him as he walked slowly up and down the beach in the dark.

"I don't know how to do this, Dylan," I said.

He didn't answer.

"I don't know how to leave you," I said to the silence. Then

Gerry's outline appeared beside me and the gentle heat of his body warmed my arm as he, too, stood beside Dylan.

Gerry picked up his stick and broke it in half. "I'm scared, Ben."

"Me too, Gerry." I stooped down to look him level in the eye and rubbed his head. "You need a haircut, buddy."

He nodded stiffly. "You too."

"Take care of Dylan."

"Okay."

Then I hugged him. I wrapped him up in my arms and picked him up and pressed his head against my shoulder. I felt his little skinny arms go around my neck and his hair stick in my face. I felt the bones in his butt where my arm held him up. Then he wrapped his sandy legs around my waist and shuddered, and I knew that was a sob he didn't want me to see.

So I held Gerry and looked at Dylan and the night closed over us and they slept. I knew that in the morning I would be strong enough. In the morning I would be able to go because I loved them and I had no other choice.

"I love you," I said to their sleeping heads. "I love you. I need you. I couldn't leave you if it wasn't so."

HOME

CHAPTER THIRTY-NINE

I DON'T REMEMBER MUCH of this part. I only remember holding Gerry before I left and pressing his head into my shoulder. I remember pushing the dinghy out through the waves and the way the mast I'd rigged looked like it would fall over. I remember some prayers without words and some crying. The sun was shining too brightly and I told Gerry to stay out of it as much as he could. I saw the sand on his toes. I saw his toenails needing trimming. I touched him again, and then I pushed the dinghy out to sea.

If I say he looked so small there on the beach watching me leave, somebody would say, "Oh, that's been said a million times before." But for me, it was the first time I had left him like that and it was my whole heart that said it. "He's so small. He's too small. This shouldn't be. God, this shouldn't be."

Behind him was the clump of trees and the tent where Dylan was lying—Dylan so brave and smart. His leg was turning red and blue, and he was the one telling me what to do. I had to leave Dylan lying there and knowing—in a way that Gerry was too little to know—what this good-bye and this waving and then this turning out to sea could mean. What it probably meant.

All I can really remember after that is my own sobs and the sound of the shirttail sail luffing while I steered a course due west. I cried when I took my sip of water. I cried when I ate the fish. I cried when the sun set. I hated myself for crying and I hated myself for leaving and I hated myself for being afraid to leave. When it was dark, I lay down in the dinghy. The water in the bottom sloshed around me. There was still a faint smell of gas from the lost engine. I closed my eyes against the sight of that ridiculous mast and sail. Then I opened them and saw a sea of foreign stars.

This was a sky Dylan had never explained to me. Even so, lying in the dinghy with the whole night sky curving from horizon to horizon over me, I felt sturdied by the stars. For a second I was lifted into space. I was shining there with them, suspended and floating free. I looked back, and there rocking on the ocean, alone and huddled down in the hard dinghy bottom, was a boy who used to be me. And just beyond the curve of the velvet, star-studded horizon was an island with waves lapping the shore and lizards feeding in the dark and two boys nesting in the sand under a rotting tent of sail. The beauty of it all—the stars, the velvet, the lapping waves, the boys—it stung me. My mind reached out to grab something, something I needed to hold. But I missed. And it was gone.

I tumbled away from space, knocking my knee against the dinghy's rough side and pinned down by a vision of Gerry, screaming square-mouthed and terrified beside Dylan's cold body while the Earth turned and they slipped away, slipped away, and disappeared. "Ben!" Gerry's voice was crying. "Ben. Come back!"

I reached for the tiller. I pulled in the sail. The bow swung slowly through the wind. I eased out the sail until I was heading east. Due east. Back to the island. I had to go home to my brothers.

Then I closed my eyes. I squeezed them hard.

"No!" I said to myself, and turned the boat back around. West. Due west. Until I was sailing away again, leaving my brothers behind once more.

The sky grew light. The gentle pearl of a dawn at sea touched the horizon, and the sky went from flat gray to mauve to aqua to transparent blue. The sun inched in a burning arc overhead. I kept the dinghy pointed straight along its path. As the sun set in a torrid orange glow, the dinghy was headed directly toward its center, creeping across the tranquil sea.

I lost the sun. I found the Pole Star. I kept it hard to starboard. I pressed down on the pictures springing up in my head. I slept. I dreamed. I woke. I slept. I lost myself in my life. I was five, licking a lemon sucker and watching Mom fold clothes. I was old, looking at my gnarled hand pick at an edge of cloth and listening to someone say, "Dad? Dad?" Then I was awake and running and falling. Only I was asleep and the voice was out on the ocean.

Then I was really awake with the call echoing in my ears.

I sat up in the dinghy, banging my elbows on the seat. "Dad!" I yelled back at the sea. "Dad! Where are you?"

I knelt and leaned as far out as I could.

"Dad!" My voice cracked. "Mom!" There was no answer. "For God's sake," I sobbed. "Where are you?"

I reached deep into the ocean, desperately paddling toward the lost voice. Then I remembered and I sat back and held my face in my dripping hands. Slowly the sun rose on a wide, empty sea.

Then suddenly, around noon, I saw the boat. She was so near. How could I not have seen her before? She was a deep-sea fishing boat, and she was coming toward me.

I stood up in the dinghy. I screamed. I waved my arms. I was thinking about Dylan and Gerry. I was praying they were still alive. So I stood up in the dinghy and screamed and waved my arms.

I can see it now like it was a movie in super-sharp focus. I see the bow gently pushing through the waves. I see the captain at the helm looking out at me and then his face changing.

What did he see? The dinghy with a mast rigged from a spinnaker pole and a sail cut with a knife from a rag of a jib.

And me standing there waving and screaming—skin burned to deep red, hair like dried seaweed, clothes streaked in salt.

He was shouting. I thought he was calling to me and I was yelling back, "Dylan and Gerry are on the island. They're waiting for me. Dylan is hurt. Gerry is too small." I stood there in the dinghy, waving and yelling and thinking that I had to make them hear over the engine noise. They had to see I was desperate.

Now I know, though, that he had cut the engines back to idle and that all the men who had hired the boat for that day were rushing to see me. The captain was telling me to sit down but I wouldn't. Then they lowered their dinghy and the captain left the helm with his mate and came to me because they were afraid that if their big boat bumped my dinghy I'd fall over and drown.

So he came over in the dinghy and he reached out and took the gunwale of my boat. His hand was strong and brown and his fingernails were dirty. His beard was flecked with gray and his eyes were deep brown. He looked at me and he said, "Sit down, son. It's gonna be all right now."

So I did. They took me aboard. One of the fishermen pulled out his handkerchief to wipe the tears off my face. One of them gave me water. They brought me in from the sun. They tied the dinghy to the boat. Somehow they made sense of what I was saying.

The captain was on the radio calling for help. I heard him saying "search" and "doctor" and I thought I heard him saying, "We'll get him to the nearest port right away." So I tried to untie my dinghy and get back in, and I was telling them about Dylan and Gerry and the voices in the sea. But they held me like in a wrestling match and looked at one another, and then the captain shouted to the mate and the boat turned around. Due east. Toward the island. Toward my brothers.

The mate gunned the engines and they let me go. The water flew away from the bow and our wake spread out behind us like a widening fan. I stood in the bow pulpit as the boat tore through the waves. I screamed at the ocean, "I'm coming back. I'm bringing help. I love you. Don't die. For God's sake, don't die."

We found the island two hours later. The captain radioed the position. We lowered his dinghy and motored in. The sun was still high but the beach was empty.

I had expected to see Gerry running up and down the beach waving to us. I had imagined splashing through the waves and grabbing him up and carrying him laughing and crying to where Dylan was waiting.

But no one was there. The captain was watching me. "Sure this is the place, son?"

I nodded. Of course. I would remember it when I was dead. When we beached the dinghy, the sand felt like home.

My feet walked toward the tent where Dylan had lain. The leaves of the sea grapes rattled. I saw a lizard slither under a fallen palm frond. Then I saw my brothers. They were lying there, side by side, Dylan on his back and Gerry on his stomach. Blankie was spread across their legs and Gerry's arm was flung across Dylan's chest. They were facing each other. They lay as still as death.

I fell on my knees.

The captain touched my shoulder. "Son—" he said.

I heard myself moan.

Then Gerry turned and sat up in one fluid movement. He saw me. He pushed the hair away from his eyes. He smiled.

"Dylan's better, Ben," he said. "He says my name again." His little hand touched Dylan's shoulder. "Dylan?" he said gently. "Ben's here."

Then Dylan turned too. Slowly. You could see it hurt him to move. His smile was ragged and out of focus. "I knew you'd come back," he said. "Didn't I tell you, Gerry? You needn't have cried so much." Dylan tried to push himself to sit. Then he fainted and collapsed onto the sand.

CHAPTER FORTY

SUDDENLY EVERYTHING WAS people and moving. I kept grabbing Gerry and trying to put him in my lap. I wanted to count his ribs or do "spider up your back." I wanted to knock Dylan on the shoulder or rub his hair up like Einstein. But we couldn't stay close to each other. A seaplane came for us, and I watched our island disappear. The viselike rocks, the waving spinnaker, the secret beach—they all spun away, and another island rose on the horizon, one with an airstrip, a marina, a town, and a hospital. They put us in baths. They fed us. They hurried Dylan away for surgery then brought him back stretched in a web of traction. When he opened his eyes, his voice was thick with drugs, but I understood him. "I knew you'd come back," he said. "I knew it."

"I tried," I said. "I love you, Dylan." Then the nurse came

and hushed me. With her hand firm on my arm, she walked me back to the room where Gerry lay sleeping. I climbed in my bed and pulled up the clean sheet. They had told me we had been on the island almost three months. Now we were here. Now Dylan would get well, and Gerry would forget. Now I would take care of them. I lay in bed and I planned it all and I felt strong.

Two days later, they let us stay with Dylan all day. At night we went back to our room. Gerry wanted stories. I didn't know any, so he made me sit on his bed and hold one corner of Blankie while he fell asleep with another corner pressed against his cheek. When he was quiet, I crept back to Dylan's room.

"How's Gerry?" he asked.

I shrugged. "He's scared. He doesn't want me to leave. He has nightmares."

"Nightmares," Dylan echoed. "Me too."

"We all do," I said. "But we'll be okay. I'm going to take care of us now, Dylan. I'm old enough. I'm almost seventeen."

"Really?" His eyes were closing.

"I'm going to fish, Dylan. And we'll get a little house here. A white one, maybe with green shutters. And one of those bushes out front—boogin-something."

"Bougainvillea," he murmured.

"Yeah, that. I'll take care of you. We'll be okay, Dylan. Just us. We'll be okay." When he didn't answer, I straightened his sheet, turned out the light, and left.

The next afternoon we were sitting in Dylan's room, making spitballs and shooting them with the straw from Dylan's lunch tray. Gerry was in my lap. I was teaching him how to aim, saying, "Go with your gut, Gerry." Dylan was talking about projectile angles and speed of launch. We were laughing, and Gerry still couldn't hit the same spot twice.

Someone knocked on the door, and Dad walked in.

No one said anything. We just looked.

Then Gerry left my lap and went to Dad. "Oh, Daddy," he said. Dad reached down and picked him up. "Ben said you'd come," Gerry said quietly, and pressed his face against Dad's shoulder.

"My boys. My boys," Dad said, and rocked Gerry in his arms and cried.

Then Dylan's IV started to beep. I reached up and pushed the button the way the nurse had taught us. She must have been just outside the door because she came immediately. She changed the medicine bag. She chatted cheerily. Dad smiled at her and wiped his face. Then she left.

"I thought you were dead," I said.

"And I thought you—" Dad started, but then his face twisted and he was quiet.

"You had the EPIRB," Dylan said.

"It saved me," Dad said.

"Instead of us," I said.

Then we were all quiet again. "I'll tell you my story," Dad finally said. "When you're ready, you tell me yours." His story wasn't very long. He said it was an accident. The night had been quiet. He had been thinking too much, he said. The coffee was making him nervous. And the thinking.

"Actually," he said, and paused. "I was thinking about your mother." He shook his head. "I decided to do a safety check, a quick walk around to stretch my legs." So he unhooked his safety harness from his life jacket and went forward. He started at the anchor and worked his way to the stern.

Of course everything was fine. We had done it all exactly right. We always did. It was ridiculous that he would do a check in the middle of the night.

"The moon was brilliant," he said. "I decided I could even check the emergency pack. It would be easy to see. There was plenty of time." He untied the dinghy and lifted it slightly. The pack came almost out, then snagged on the dinghy seat. He tugged harder. His grip slipped. He stumbled backwards. As he fell over, he grabbed the lifeline. The pack slid loose, flopped to the edge of the boat, and then fell in. He grabbed it with his left hand and held the lifeline with his right hand, his injured hand.

He called out, he said. He was almost beside Dylan, except for the fiberglass hull between them. "But you know Dylan," he said. "He can sleep through anything." He shouted again and his grip loosened. Then a wave tore him away from the boat. He watched the boat sail away. Five knots, steady wind, perfect steering. The boat was out of sight before he remembered to be glad he had on his life jacket.

He was staring at his hands.

"You tell a good story," I said.

He looked up at me quickly then continued. He drifted for a long time, he said, before he remembered he had the EPIRB. Then he floated on the pack, holding the EPIRB and watching the clouds. By the time we woke up, we were already miles away from him and the storm was building.

I felt sick listening to him tell it all.

The wind was blowing the crests off the waves when the rescue boat finally located him. He tried to get them to look for us, but they refused. Their boat couldn't go head on into the forty-foot waves they were reporting. "Sorry, sir," the sailor had said. "We'll try to radio. That's the best we can do." Dad said something about being cold and drinking coffee. Something about fifty-knot winds and forty-foot waves. Something about staring out windows blinded by horizontal rain.

All I heard was the sound of the wind screaming through the stays and the explosion of the mainsail as we skidded down the front of that wave. All I could see was the waves breaking behind us as high up as the top of the mast and as black as tornado clouds. And then Dylan like a yellow caterpillar unfolding to take the helm and Gerry alone on the floor, wearing a red life jacket and clutching Blankie.

Dad rented a room in Miami. There were broadcasts and airplanes. There were newspaper stories and sightings. But they couldn't find us. Nobody imagined how far the storm had blown us. They never even came close to our island. After a month, the authorities closed the search, but Dad kept on. He went back to the Bahamas and took the ferries among the islands. He asked everybody he saw but everybody agreed—after a storm like that, the most likely place to find us was at the bottom of the sea.

After another month, Dad went home. He rented an apartment. He started teaching again. "'My life closed twice before its close,'" he read aloud, but the students didn't understand. He turned the page and cried out to them, "'Do not go gentle into that good night. Rage, rage against the dying of the light.'" Then the class was over. The students yawned and stretched. They closed their books. They left.

At night he stared at the TV or at the ceiling, depending on whether or not he was trying to sleep. Until yesterday—when they called.

"And so I came," he said. "To bring you home."

I laughed. "Home?" I said. "Where's that?"

They all looked at me. I twisted in my chair and looked out the window. There was that blazing island sun. There was the bougainvillea. There was a lizard clinging to the screen and tasting the hot, damp air. I thumped the lizard off the screen into the bushes. I crossed the room and stood in front of Dad. I looked him level in the eye and it surprised us both.

"You've grown," he said.

"Yeah. I got hair on my chest while you were gone."

Gerry reached out and tried to pull up my shirt. "Really, Ben? Let me see."

I turned away. "It's just a way of talking, Gerry."

"It's time to think about a car," Dad said, and smiled.

"I don't want a car."

"I called Andrew," Dad said. "He's looking forward—"

I pushed Gerry's hair away from his eyes. "It's hot in here, bud," I said. "I'm going to take a walk."

"Ben—" Dad was saying as I walked past him and out the door.

Then the small, close room was behind me and the low, cool corridor and the swinging door, and I was outside. I leaned against the concrete-block wall and felt my heart racing. I imagined Dad coming to find me. I couldn't talk to him. I couldn't listen to his voice. I couldn't stand to let my eyes touch his face or his hands or his shoes.

I had said I would walk, so I would walk, but suddenly the island seemed small. There was nothing but the town itself with its hospital and houses and marina all bunched up along the beach and then the long, white, glaring road that led to the crushed-coral airstrip about a mile out of town. A taxi was parked at the grocery store. The driver sat with his door open and his feet rubbing on the dusty road. He sipped at a soda in a paper bag and talked with a man sitting on a bench. Outside one house, a woman was braiding a little girl's hair, and a baby wearing just a diaper was mashing an acorn into the dust.

I paused in the shade of some tall casuarinas growing near the shore. I rolled acorns into a pile with my toes and watched a clutch of chickens scratching close to me, then scattering away. I was turning to keep walking when Dad found me. He sat down on an empty oil drum a few feet away. I picked up a handful of acorns and pitched one across the road into the dirty edge of the sea.

"I came to get you," he said. "They're making us something special for dinner."

"I'm not hungry."

"Dylan and Gerry are waiting. We need to go back."

"I said I'm not hungry."

He stopped talking for a minute then said, "You're angry with me, aren't you?" He rubbed the rusty edge of the drum, then studied the orange spot on his fingertip.

"No," I said, "it's worse than that." I turned away from him and squeezed the acorns in my hand. "I hate you," I said, and threw the whole handful into the ocean. They fell like a shower of bombs. "I hate you," I said again, and started to walk away.

"Ben!" I heard Dad's feet behind me. His hand gripped my arm. "Look at me!" He spun me to face him and grabbed my other arm.

"Let go," I said.

"No. I want you to tell me what's wrong."

"You want to know what's wrong? Okay, I'll tell you. You tried to kill yourself. Why did you do that?"

He dropped my arms and stepped back.

"Then Gerry almost drowned and Dylan almost died. And even Mom. You made her—"

"So," he said. He was shaking. "So." He swallowed hard. "I see." He looked quickly toward the dirty beach and then back at me. "You left before I could tell you," he said. "A special plane is flying in tomorrow. We can roll Dylan's bed right onto the plane—IV, traction, and all. They're taking us to the hospital in Miami. In a few days, we'll be able to go all the way home."

"Home." I spit the word back at him. "You like that word now, don't you?" I looked toward the sea, then back at him. I shook my head. "I won't go," I said. "Not with you." Then I walked away.

CHAPTER FORTY-ONE

WHEN I LEFT Dad, I walked to the marina and sat at the end of the pier so all I could see was the ocean and the darkening sky. The wind lifted my hair off my neck. It would have made a perfect reach south. Two slips behind me, three guys loaded provisions on a cruising yacht. They were leaving tomorrow for Hawaii through the Panama Canal to deliver the boat to its new owner. They were shorthanded and they were worried.

We would have loved that. Dylan, Gerry, and me, island hopping to the Canal. Dylan would tell us about the stars and Gerry would play in the cockpit. I would hold the tiller and watch the sails. We would see whales. We could have done that. Or I could have taken care of them in the little house. But Dad came back. He just walked in and said, "Let's go," ordering us around exactly the way he had done before.

I had said I wouldn't go with Dad. I meant it.

I walked across the dock to where the guys were talking. "I can help," I said. I lied about my age, but I told the truth about how much I'd sailed. They were glad to have me. Seven thirty tomorrow morning, they said. Don't bring much stuff.

I shook hands with my new mates. *That was easy,* I thought. I had a job now and could take care of myself. I didn't need Dad for anything. I sat on the bench by the grocery store and clenched my jaw tight and waited. The only thing I needed now was to tell Dylan and Gerry good-bye.

When it was late, I walked back to the hospital just in time to see Dad leaving with Gerry in his arms. When Gerry rested his head on Dad's shoulder and Dad rubbed his fingers in Gerry's hair, I suddenly remembered the sharp feel of the bones in Gerry's butt weighing on my arms and the softness of his cheek against my collarbone. I felt the slightly damp place his tears left on my shirt. I felt that long night stretch out before me, and I was scared all over again. Scared and helpless and responsible.

Then Dad and Gerry were gone, and I crept to Dylan's room. The lights were turned down for him to sleep, but as I opened the door, the hall light caught in his open eyes. The door closed behind me, and the room was dark again, lit only by the light through the window. Dylan held out his hand. I took it. It was still smaller than mine—much smaller—but I felt stronger holding it.

"You didn't come back for dinner," he said.

"I wasn't hungry."

"Dad's bringing a special plane tomorrow," he said. "We're going home."

I nodded. "Dylan." I let go of his hand and pressed my palms against my forehead. "I came to tell you—I'm not going. I won't go with Dad."

The pillow rustled as Dylan turned his head toward me.

"But it was an accident, Ben. I was right."

"It's not just that. It's everything—the boat, the Bahamas, Bermuda." I took a deep breath. "Look at you, Dylan. Your leg. You almost—" I stopped. "And Gerry. The nightmares. Dad hurt you, Dylan. He hurt Gerry." I shook the bed rail and Dylan winced. I let go and walked to the door.

"Wait," Dylan said.

I opened the door and looked back. The light from the hall lay in a long rectangle across the room. I could see a duffel bag full of new clothes sitting on the floor.

"I just signed on as crew for a yacht delivery to Hawaii," I said. "We leave in the morning. I'm going to see Hawaii, Dylan. And maybe Tahiti. Who knows? It'll be exciting. I'll let you know where I am. I'll always let you know where I am."

"You're really leaving?" He pushed himself up on his elbows. "Don't go."

As I walked out, the door closed soundlessly behind me.

I walked the dark streets searching for Dad's motel, and then there it was, low and dark with all the rooms opening onto a patio. Through the opened curtains of one window, I saw Gerry sleeping alone on one side of a double bed. Dad was gone. When I tried the door, it wasn't locked. I slipped inside.

Gerry breathed gently and steadily. When I bent over him I could smell the soap of his shower. When I touched his cheek, it was damp with sweat. Carefully I pulled Blankie off his neck and laid it across his open hands. In his sleep, he moved slightly, then closed his hands on the worn white cloth and raised it to his face.

The floor was a mess. Several open duffel bags spilled across the straw rug. An unopened pack of Batman underwear lay beside one bag. A pile of little-kid books had fallen under a table. A box of markers and a pad of paper sat on Gerry's nightstand. I picked them up to write a note, but I didn't know what to say. In the end, I wrote three words, *Good-bye, little Noogie.* I signed it *Love, Ben.*

When I turned away from Gerry, the door was open and Dad was standing just inside the darkness. "I've been waiting for you," he said. "The other bed is yours, and that bag of gear." He pointed across the room to a large, unopened duffel bag.

I crossed the room and unzipped it. On top lay five magazines, the latest issue of every car magazine there was. I felt around inside. Two adjustable caps, clothes, and on the bottom some kind of electronic game and CDs. I couldn't tell exactly what it all was just by feeling, but I knew Dad had brought me everything I needed for my new job. I hoisted the bag to my shoulder and shoved past Dad into the cooler air of the night.

"Wait," he said, following me and closing the door quietly behind him. "We have to talk." He sat in one of the chairs on the patio and gestured for me to take the other.

I put my bag on the table and stood in the dark.

"Dylan had the nurse call from the hospital," he said. "You can't do this, you know. You can't just—"

"You can't stop me," I interrupted.

Dad closed his eyes and rubbed his forehead hard with his fingertips. "Ben," he said, "I didn't try to kill myself. Why would I do that?"

"Why would you do a safety check in the middle of the night?"

"I was stupid."

I shrugged.

He drew in breath slowly. "Okay." He looked away. "I did think about it—killing myself, I mean. Right after your mother's accident, I thought about it a lot." He closed his eyes. "When I went overboard, I knew all I had to do was let go of the EPIRB. It would have been easy."

He looked up at me and his voice turned hard. "But I didn't let go. I didn't *want* to let go."

I shifted my weight in the dark. I wondered if there was blood on the ledge where Dylan had lain. I wondered what had happened to the life jacket Dad had been wearing when he fell into the sea. I wondered who was riding Mom's bicycle these days.

"And you think what happened to your mother is my fault," Dad said. "I know what you mean by that, and it's not fair." His fingers marked the width of the chair arm. "It took me a long time to figure that out," he said. "But I did, and I can tell you it's not fair."

He looked at me again. "I loved your mother, Ben. I love

her now. Her face. Her voice. The way she laughed at me." He shifted his gaze to the bushes at the edge of the patio. "The way she needed me," he went on, "sometimes just to hold her."

He looked at his hand gripping the chair arm. "The way you reach for the wall sometimes," he said, "just to steady yourself—like when you stump your toe and the pain makes you dizzy."

He let go of the chair arm and breathed in deeply. "And I needed her," he said. "When she died, there was nothing to hold me up, and I fell."

He paused then looked up at me. "You've been so brave. You saved them."

"We saved each other," I said.

"Dylan told me everything. And Gerry's been asking for you all night."

I reached for my bag. "I'll be writing them," I said.

"But you can't leave them. They'll miss you."

"They're tough. They'll be okay."

"And you'll miss—"

"No," I said quickly. "No, I won't."

Dad sat still in his chair. I fingered the strap on my shoulder. The sounds of the sleeping town rose up around us. Car tires crunched on the street. A door shut somewhere in the hotel. The breeze pushed an old palm frond against the side of the building. We watched it slap the concrete helplessly with one worn brown leaf.

Dad stood. "One more thing," he said. He reached into his pocket and held something out to me.

I put the bag down again and took it. It was a soft, silky square. Like a tiny pillow. I turned it over in my hands. A faint scent came off it. Mom. Mom's sachet.

"Where did you get this?" My voice was sharp.

"The boxes."

"Where are the boxes?"

"At my place."

I breathed in the fading perfume. I swallowed. "You didn't give away her stuff?"

"Of course not. Why would I do that?"

"I thought—" The scent was making me dizzy. "Why did you bring this to me?"

"I brought one for each of you."

"Why?"

"Because I couldn't bring your mother."

I turned my back on him and walked away.

As I walked, the sidewalk tilted up and down under my feet. I felt the lump of silk in my hand and the shaking inside me. I found myself again beside the sea. I lay down on the little sandy beach and the trembling stilled. I held the sachet to my cheek.

The stars were swimming in the sky. I blinked again and again, and they came into focus. I had them memorized. I could see them from the bow of *Chrysalis*, from the beach of our island, from the bottom of the dinghy. The pinpricks of light glittering like broken glass, spilling in mysterious patterns across the night sky.

Dylan had finally made me understand that the stars don't change. We do. We see them from a tilting, spinning earth circling the sun. We can see them only when the sun is behind us. And even then we see only that tiny portion of the vast universe that is directly above the pinpoint of space we are pointed toward at that single moment in time.

The earth had shifted and I could see Orion again with his belt of three brilliant stars. There were the Pleiades too, shining together like a dusting of silver on the sky.

Pleiades means "the sisters."

We never had any sisters. Mom said once that someday our wives would be her daughters. She told us to love them because without love, she said, you are just another person. But with love, you are a power. I remember she was holding my hand on one side of her and Dylan's on the other and Gerry was sitting in her lap. She had been trying to explain about the baby who had died, the brother who would have come after Gerry. Then she was telling us about how much she loved us and Dad. And then she was holding our hands and crying a little, and we were watching.

What if she knew about it all? I thought. What would she say? What would anyone say? It had been awful, but it was over. We had survived. Tomorrow Dad and Dylan and Gerry would leave on a plane, and I would leave on a boat. Finally I would be free. I would be alone and empty and free.

CHAPTER FORTY-TWO

WHEN I WOKE up, I was wet with dew and sticky with sand. I sat up in the early sun, still holding the sachet, and realized I had left the duffel bag sitting on the patio table. My big dramatic exit, and I had screwed it up. I would have to go empty-handed. As I walked up to the marina, I saw the taxi driver standing by his cab and sipping coffee from a white mug. Just as I recognized Gerry's blond head in the backseat of the cab, Dad walked out of the marina office.

"There you are!" Dad said when he saw me. His face was tight. I could see he hadn't slept all night.

Gerry turned and looked through the open window at me.

"Hi, Ben," he called, his face breaking into a happy, little-kid grin.

I smiled back.

"We're going home today," Gerry said.

I nodded a little. The cabdriver slid back into his seat and shut his door.

"The ambulance is already on its way to the plane," Dad said. "Once Dylan's out of the hospital, he needs to get to Miami right away. We can't wait. We have to hurry." He shook his head. Then he turned to me. "Please, Ben," he said.

I looked away.

"It was a mistake," Dad said. "I should have—"

The sun grew hotter. The silence stretched thin.

Dad pulled the duffel bag out from beside Gerry and handed it to me. Gerry watched. The smile on his face was changing.

Dad took out his wallet. He gave me four hundred-dollar bills. "That might be enough for a plane ticket," he said. "If it's not, I'll wire it. Just telephone. I'll—"

The halyards rang like bells and the dockworkers called to one another. I shoved the money into my shirt pocket.

"Please," he said again.

I looked at the road.

"Shake?" Dad finally asked, and held out his hand.

I took it. He held my hand a long, long minute.

"Good luck," he mumbled. Then he climbed quickly into the cab beside Gerry. He spoke to the driver. The car started.

Gerry spun in his seat and looked at me out the back window as the car drove away. "What about Ben?" His mouth turned into a black square. "What about Ben?" He pressed his hands flat against the inside of the window. His palms went white. "What about Ben?" he cried, and the car slowly turned a corner on crunching tires.

Then I was standing alone on the dock with my bag hanging on my back. I touched my shirt pocket. It was stiff. That was the money—and Mom's picture. She didn't look as good as when I first stuck her in the pages of my diesel engine book, but she was still there. I took her out and looked at her while I held the sachet to my cheek. I noticed she had Gerry's eyes and Dylan's mouth. I was the one who looked like Dad.

I squinted my eyes against the sun's glare and felt my insides swell with missing Mom. We never got to tell her goodbye. We never got to say how much we loved her. Now all I could think about was how bad it hurt to have lost her. I closed my eyes and stretched my jaw and slid Mom back into my pocket.

And then, like turning a book of blank pages and suddenly seeing a picture, I saw the golden day again. I felt that cool breeze and heard that gentle ocean and saw my brothers' bunny butts hopping off into the water while I sat there watching them and trying helplessly to remember something. My stupid brain had been like an engine trying to start, trying to turn over. A chug and silence. A chug and silence.

Then standing there in the painful sunshine with my new ship in the harbor and slipping Mom's picture into my pocket under the crisp bills, I felt the engine start, and the sound I heard was Dad. I heard Dad on the night after the baby died.

I had given up getting a drink and had left Mom crying and Dad murmuring in the dark kitchen. When Mom slowly climbed the stairs and went to bed, I lay still, pretending sleep. Even later, I listened as Dad checked the doors downstairs and then came up himself. I heard him look in on Gerry and then come into our room. I heard him adjust Dylan's covers and stand quietly for a moment by his bed. Then he came to me. He touched my hair. I turned over and saw him standing there in the half dark.

He sat down on my bed and looked out into the lighted hallway. "You know, Ben," he said, "I didn't want children." He turned and looked down at me. "I wanted freedom. At least that's what I said." He touched my arm. "But really I was afraid." He picked up my hand. "How can anyone be a dad? How can you do all the things you need to do—all day every day for a lifetime?"

He put my hand down and patted it. "And I knew," he said quietly, "there would be days like today. From the day I first held you, I have been afraid of a day like today."

He leaned back against the headboard and closed his eyes. "I heard you on the stairs," he said. "You saw us in the kitchen tonight, didn't you?"

I nodded on my pillow.

"You saw us crying. You know we're sad." He paused. "I'll tell you a story."

He folded his hands in his lap and I closed my eyes.

"Once upon a time, there was a man who was afraid. He felt safe in his study, but he was lonely. On an island nearby lived a beautiful woman. Sharks circled her island night and day, never resting. The man had a choice. He could close his door, learn not to think of her, and stay lonely. Or he could go outside and jump. He jumped."

Dad stopped. I opened my eyes and waited.

Then he went on. "It's been that way with each of you," he said. "The knowing about the sharks and the jumping anyway. Tonight and for a long time to come, your mom and I will be hurting. But we are not sorry we jumped."

I turned slightly under my covers to face him. The light from the hall cast his silhouette in strong relief. He looked toward me. He took my hand again.

"When you are a man—" he began, then stopped.

"What?" I asked. "Will I jump?"

He put my hand down again and stood. "I don't know, Ben." He bent and kissed me lightly on the forehead. "That's your part of the story."

Then he walked away, and I lay in my bed, listening to Dylan breathe until I finally fell asleep.

Now, standing in the sun, I heard Dad again. My dad. My only dad.

The CDs broke as I dropped my bag on the cement dock.

Then I was running.

And that, I tell Gerry, is the end of the story. We went home. We found a new house. We unpacked the boxes.

And when April came around again, we bought a new boat. We docked it at the lake, and now every chance we get, we take it sailing.

Just us—skimming the lake, riding the wind.

A boat. A dad. And three brothers.

ACKNOWLEDGMENTS

I would like to thank Don K. Haycraft, Stephen and Ann Marlowe, Captain James E. Herlong, Dr. Stephen W. Hales, and Captain Cliff Block for generously sharing their expertise and support as the adventures of the Byron family unfolded.

—M. H. Herlong